PZ
3
.R284
Cr12

Remington,
Frederic

Crooked trails.

CROOKED TRAILS

by

Frederic Remington

LIBRARY
Herkimer County Community College

LITERATURE HOUSE / GREGG PRESS
Upper Saddle River, N. J.

Republished in 1970 by
LITERATURE HOUSE
an imprint of The Gregg Press
121 Pleasant Avenue
Upper Saddle River, N. J. 07458

Standard Book Number—8398-1753-3
Library of Congress Card—72-104547

Printed in United States of America

TEXAS RANGERS HOLDING UP CHAPPARAL BANDITS

CROOKED TRAILS

WRITTEN AND
ILLUSTRATED BY

FREDERIC REMINGTON
AUTHOR OF "PONY TRACKS"

LONDON AND NEW YORK
HARPER & BROTHERS PUBLISHERS
1898

CONTENTS

ILLUSTRATIONS

v

ILLUSTRATIONS

CROOKED TRAILS

HOW THE LAW
GOT INTO THE CHAPARRAL

"You have heard about the Texas Rangers?"
said the Deacon to me one night in the San Antonio Club. "Yes? Well, come up to my rooms,
and I will introduce you to one of the old originals
—dates 'way back in the 'thirties'—there aren't
many of them left now—and if we can get him to
talk, he will tell you stories that will make your
eyes hang out on your shirt front."

We entered the Deacon's cosey bachelor apart-
ments, where I was introduced to Colonel "Rip"
Ford, of the old-time Texas Rangers. I found
him a very old man, with a wealth of snow-white
hair and beard—bent, but not withered. As he
sunk on his stiffened limbs into the arm-chair, we
disposed ourselves quietly and almost reverentially,
while we lighted cigars. We began the approaches
by which we hoped to loosen the history of a wild
past from one of the very few tongues which can

A   I

still wag on the days when the Texans, the Comanches, and the Mexicans chased one another
over the plains of Texas, and shot and stabbed to
find who should inherit the land.

Through the veil of tobacco smoke the ancient
warrior spoke his sentences slowly, at intervals, as
his mind gradually separated and arranged the
details of countless fights. His head bowed in
thought; anon it rose sharply at recollections, and
as he breathed, the shouts and lamentations of
crushed men—the yells and shots—the thunder of
horses' hoofs—the full fury of the desert combats
came to the pricking ears of the Deacon and me.

We saw through the smoke the brave young
faces of the hosts which poured into Texas to war
with the enemies of their race. They were clad in
loose hunting-frocks, leather leggings, and broad
black hats; had powder-horns and shot-pouches
hung about them; were armed with bowie-knives,
Mississippi rifles, and horse-pistols; rode Spanish
ponies, and were impelled by Destiny to conquer,
like their remote ancestors, " the godless hosts of
Pagan " who " came swimming o'er the Northern
Sea."

" Rip " Ford had not yet acquired his front
name in 1836, when he enlisted in the famous
Captain Jack Hayes's company of Rangers, which
was fighting the Mexicans in those days, and also

trying incidentally to keep from being eaten up by the Comanches.

Said the old Colonel : " A merchant from our country journeyed to New York, and Colonel Colt, who was a friend of his, gave him two five-shooters —pistols they were, and little things. The merchant in turn presented them to Captain Jack Hayes. The captain liked them so well that he did not rest till every man jack of us had two apiece.

" Directly," mused the ancient one, with a smile of pleasant recollection, " we had a fight with the Comanches—up here above San Antonio. Hayes had fifteen men with him—he was doubling about the country for Indians. He found ' sign,' and after cutting their trail several times he could see that they were following him. Directly the Indians overtook the Rangers — there were seventy-five Indians. Captain Hayes—bless his memory! —said, ' They are fixin' to charge us, boys, and we must charge them.' There were never better men in this world than Hayes had with him," went on the Colonel with pardonable pride ; " and mind you, he never made a fight without winning.

" We charged, and in the fracas killed thirty-five Indians—only two of our men were wounded—so you see the five-shooters were pretty good weapons. Of course they wa'n't any account compared

3

with these modern ones, because they were too small, but they did those things. Just after that Colonel Colt was induced to make bigger ones for us, some of which were half as long as your arm.

"Hayes? Oh, he was a surveyor, and used to go out beyond the frontiers about his work. The Indians used to jump him pretty regular; but he always whipped them, and so he was available for a Ranger captain. About then—let's see," and here the old head bobbed up from his chest, where it had sunk in thought—"there was a commerce with Mexico just sprung up, but this was later—it only shows what that man Hayes used to do. The bandits used to waylay the traders, and they got very bad in the country. Captain Hayes went after them—he struck them near Lavade, and found the Mexicans had more than twice as many men as he did; but he caught them napping, charged them afoot—killed twenty-five of them, and got all their horses."

"I suppose, Colonel, you have been charged by a Mexican lancer?" I inquired.

"Oh yes, many times," he answered.

"What did you generally do?"

"Well, you see, in those days I reckoned to be able to hit a man every time with a six-shooter at one hundred and twenty-five yards," explained the

A BEARER OF CIVILIZATION

old gentleman—which no doubt meant many dead
lancers.

" Then you do not think much of a lance as a
weapon ?" I pursued.

" No ; there is but one weapon. The six-shooter
when properly handled is the only weapon—mind
you, sir, I say *properly*," and here the old eyes
blinked rapidly over the great art as he knew its
practice.

" Then, of course, the rifle has its use. Under
Captain Jack Hayes sixty of us made a raid once
after the celebrated priest - leader of the Mexicans
—Padre Jarante—which same was a devil of a fellow. We were very sleepy—had been two nights
without sleep. At San Juan every man stripped
his horse, fed, and went to sleep. We had passed
Padre Jarante in the night without knowing it.
At about twelve o'clock next day there was a ter-
rible outcry—I was awakened by shooting. The
Padre was upon us. Five men outlying stood the
charge, and went under. We gathered, and the
Padre charged three times. The third time he
was knocked from his horse and killed. Then
Captain Jack Hayes awoke, and we got in a big
casa. The men took to the roof. As the Mexicans passed we emptied a great many saddles.
As I got to the top of the *casa* I found two men
quarrelling." (Here the Colonel chuckled.) " I

5

asked what the matter was, and they were both claiming to have killed a certain Mexican who was lying dead some way off. One said he had hit him in the head, and the other said he had hit him in the breast. I advised peace until after the fight. Well—after the shooting was over and the Padre's men had had enough, we went out to the particular Mexican who was dead, and, sure enough, he was shot in the head and in the breast; so they laughed and made peace. About this time one of the spies came in and reported six hundred Mexicans coming. We made an examination of our ammunition, and found that we couldn't afford to fight six hundred Mexicans with sixty men, so we pulled out. This was in the Mexican war, and only goes to show that Captain Hayes's men could shoot all the Mexicans that could get to them if the ammunition would hold out."

" What was the most desperate fight you can remember, Colonel?"

The old man hesitated; this required a particular point of view—it was quality, not quantity, wanted now; and, to be sure, he was a connoisseur. After much study by the Colonel, during which the world lost many thrilling tales, the one which survived occurred in 1851.

" My lieutenant, Ed Burleson, was ordered to

6

THE CHARGE AND KILLING OF PADRE JARANTE

carry to San Antonio an Indian prisoner we had taken and turned over to the commanding officer at Fort McIntosh. On his return, while nearing the Nueces River, he spied a couple of Indians. Taking seven men, he ordered the balance to continue along the road. The two Indians proved to be fourteen, and they charged Burleson up to the teeth. Dismounting his men, he poured it into them from his Colt's six-shooting rifles. They killed or wounded all the Indians except two, some of them dying so near the Rangers that they could put their hands on their boots. All but one of Burleson's men were wounded—himself shot in the head with an arrow. One man had four 'dogwood switches ' * in his body, one of which was in his bowels. This man told me that every time he raised his gun to fire, the Indians would stick an arrow in him, but he said he didn't care a cent. One Indian was lying right up close, and while dying tried to shoot an arrow, but his strength failed so fast that the arrow only barely left the bowstring. One of the Rangers in that fight was a curious fellow—when young he had been captured by Indians, and had lived with them so long that he had Indian habits. In that fight he kept jumping around when loading, so as to be a bad

* Arrows.

7

target, the same as an Indian would under the circumstances, and he told Burleson he wished he had his boots off, so he could get around good "— and here the Colonel paused quizzically. " Would you call that a good fight?"

The Deacon and I put the seal of our approval on the affair, and the Colonel rambled ahead.

" In 1858 I was commanding the frontier battalion of State troops on the whole frontier, and had my camp on the Deer Fork of the Brazos. The Comanches kept raiding the settlements. They would come down quietly, working well into the white lines, and then go back a-running—driving stolen stock and killing and burning. I thought I would give them some of their own medicine. I concluded to give them a fight. I took two wagons, one hundred Rangers, and one hundred and thirteen Tahuahuacan Indians, who were friendlies. We struck a good Indian trail on a stream which led up to the Canadian. We followed it till it got hot. I camped my outfit in such a manner as to conceal my force, and sent out my scouts, who saw the Indians hunt buffalo through spyglasses. That night we moved. I sent Indians to locate the camp. They returned before day, and reported that the Indians were just a few miles ahead, whereat we moved forward. At daybreak, I remember, I was standing in the bull-

"WE STRUCK SOME BOGGY GROUND"

wagon road leading to Santa Fe and could see the Canadian River in our front—with eighty lodges just beyond. Counting four men of fighting age to a lodge, that made a possible three hundred and twenty Indians. Just at sunup an Indian came across the river on a pony. Our Indians down below raised a yell — they always get excited. The Indian heard them — it was very still then. The Indian retreated slowly, and began to ride in a circle. From where I was I could hear him puff like a deer—he was blowing the bullets away from himself—he was a medicine-man. I heard five shots from the Jagers with which my Indians were armed. The painted pony of the medicine-man jumped ten feet in the air, it seemed to me, and fell over on his rider—then five more Jagers went off, and he was dead. I ordered the Tahuahuacans out in front, and kept the Rangers out of sight, because I wanted to charge home and kind of surprise them. Pretty soon I got ready, and gave the word. We charged. At the river we struck some boggy ground and floundered around considerable, but we got through. We raised the Texas yell, and away we went. I never expect again to hear such a noise—I never want to hear it—what with the whoops of the warriors—the screaming of the women and children—our boys yelling—the shooting, and the horses just a-mixin' up and a-stam-

9

pedin' around," and the Colonel bobbed his head slowly as he continued.

"One of my men didn't know a buck from a squaw. There was an Indian woman on a pony with five children. He shot the pony—it seemed like you couldn't see that pony for little Indians. We went through the camp, and the Indians pulled out—spreading fanlike, and we a-running them. After a long chase I concluded to come back. I saw lots of Indians around in the hills. When I got back, I found Captain Ross had formed my men in line. 'What time in the morning is it?' I asked. 'Morning, hell!' says he—'it's one o'clock!' And so it was. Directly I saw an Indian coming down a hill near by, and then more Indians and more Indians—till it seemed like they wa'n't ever going to get through coming. We had struck a bigger outfit than the first one. That first Indian he bantered my men to come out single-handed and fight him. One after another, he wounded five of my Indians. I ordered my Indians to engage them, and kind of get them down in the flat, where I could charge. After some running and shooting they did this, and I turned the Rangers loose. We drove them. The last stand they made they killed one of my Indians, wounded a Ranger, but left seven of their dead in a pile. It was now nearly nightfall, and I discovered that my horses were broken down after fighting all day. I found it hard to restrain my men, they had got so heated up; but I gradually withdrew to where the fight commenced. The Indian camp was plundered. In it we found painted buffalo-robes with beads a hand deep around the edges—the finest robes I have ever seen—and heaps of goods plundered from the Santa Fe traders. On the way back I noticed a dead chief, and was for a moment astonished to find pieces of flesh cut out of him; upon looking at a Tahuahuacan warrior I saw a pair of dead hands tied behind his saddle. That night they had a cannibal feast. You see, the Tahuahuacans say that the first one of their race was brought into the world by a wolf. 'How am I to live?' said the Tahuahuacan. 'The same as we do,' said the wolf; and when they were with me, that is just about how they lived. I reckon it's necessary to tell you about the old woman who was found in our lines. She was looking at the sun and making incantations, a-cussing us out generally and elevating her voice. She said the Comanches would get even for this day's work. I directed my Indians to let her alone, but I was informed afterwards that that is just what they didn't do."

At this point the Colonel's cigar went out, and directly he followed; but this is the manner in which he told of deeds which I know would fare better at the hands of one used to phrasing and capable also of more points of view than the Colonel was used to taking. The outlines of the thing are strong, however, because the Deacon and I understood that fights were what the old Colonel had dealt in during his active life, much as other men do in stocks and bonds or wheat and corn. He had been a successful operator, and only recalled pleasantly the bull quotations. This type of Ranger is all but gone. A few may yet be found in outlying ranches. One of the most celebrated resides near San Antonio—" Big-foot Wallace " by name. He says he doesn't mind being called " Big-foot," because he is six feet two in height, and is entitled to big feet. His face is done off in a nest of white hair and beard, and is patriarchal in character. In 1836 he came out from Virginia to "take toll " of the Mexicans for killing some relatives of his in the Fannin Massacre, and he considers that he has squared his accounts; but they had him on the debit side for a while. Being captured in the Meir expedition, he walked as a prisoner to the city of Mexico, and did public work for that country with a ball-and-chain attachment for two years. The prisoners overpowered the guards and escaped on one occasion, but were overtaken by Mexican cavalry while dying of thirst in a desert. Santa Anna

PRISONERS DRAWING THEIR BEANS

ordered their "decimation," which meant that every tenth man was shot, their lot being determined by the drawing of a black bean from an earthen pot containing a certain proportion of white ones. "Big-foot" drew a white one. He was also a member of Captain Hayes's company, afterwards a captain of Rangers, and a noted Indian-fighter. Later he carried the mails from San Antonio to El Paso through a howling wilderness, but always brought it safely through—if safely can be called lying thirteen days by a water-hole in the desert, waiting for a broken leg to mend, and living meanwhile on one prairie-wolf, which he managed to shoot. Wallace was a professional hunter, who fought Indians and hated "greasers"; he belongs to the past, and has been "outspanned" under a civilization in which he has no place, and is to-day living in poverty.

The civil war left Texas under changed conditions. That and the Mexican wars had determined its boundaries, however, and it rapidly filled up with new elements of population. Broken soldiers, outlaws, poor immigrants living in bull-wagons, poured in. "Gone to Texas" had a sinister significance in the late sixties. When the railroad got to Abilene, Kansas, the cow-men of Texas found a market for their stock, and began trailing their herds up through the Indian country.

Bands of outlaws organized under the leadership of desperadoes like Wes Hardin and King Fisher. They rounded up cattle regardless of their owners' rights, and resisted interference with force. The poor man pointed to his brand in the stolen herd and protested. He was shot. The big owners were unable to protect themselves from loss. The property right was established by the six-shooter, and honest men were forced to the wall. In 1876 the property-holding classes went to the Legislature, got it to appropriate a hundred thousand dollars a year for two years, and the Ranger force was reorganized to carry the law into the chaparral. At this time many judges were in league with bandits; sheriffs were elected by the outlaws, and the electors were cattle-stealers.

The Rangers were sworn to uphold the laws of Texas and the United States. They were deputy sheriffs, United States marshals—in fact, were often vested with any and every power, even to the extent of ignoring disreputable sheriffs. At times they were judge, jury, and executioner when the difficulties demanded extremes. When a band of outlaws was located, detectives or spies were sent among them, who openly joined the desperadoes, and gathered evidence to put the Rangers on their trail. Then, in the wilderness, with only the soaring buzzard or prowling coyote to look on, the

TEXAS RANGERS

Ranger and the outlaw met to fight with tigerish ferocity to the death. Shot, and lying prone, they fired until the palsied arm could no longer raise the six-shooter, and justice was satisfied as their bullets sped. The captains had the selection of their men, and the right to dishonorably discharge at will. Only men of irreproachable character, who were fine riders and dead-shots, were taken. The spirit of adventure filled the ranks with the most prominent young men in the State, and to have been a Ranger is a badge of distinction in Texas to this day. The display of anything but a perfect willingness to die under any and all circumstances was fatal to a Ranger, and in course of time they got the *moral* on the bad man. Each one furnished his own horse and arms, while the State gave him ammunition, "grub," one dollar a day, and extra expenses. The enlistment was for twelve months. A list of fugitive Texas criminals was placed in his hands, with which he was expected to familiarize himself. Then, in small parties, they packed the bedding on their mule, they hung the handcuffs and leather thongs about its neck, saddled their riding-ponies, and threaded their way into the chaparral.

On an evening I had the pleasure of meeting two more distinguished Ranger officers — more modern types — Captains Lea Hall and Joseph

Shely; both of them big, forceful men, and loath to talk about themselves. It was difficult to associate the quiet gentlemen who sat smoking in the Deacon's rooms with what men say; for the tales of their prowess in Texas always ends, "and that don't count Mexicans, either." The bandit never laid down his gun but with his life; so the "la ley de huga"* was in force in the chaparral, and the good people of Texas were satisfied with a very short account of a Ranger's fight.

The most distinguished predecessor of these two men was a Captain McNally, who was so bent on carrying his raids to an issue that he paid no heed to national boundary-lines. He followed a band of Mexican bandits to the town of La Cueva, below Ringgold, once, and, surrounding it, demanded the surrender of the cattle which they had stolen. He had but ten men, and yet this redoubtable warrior surrounded a town full of bandits and Mexican soldiers. The Mexican soldiers attacked the Rangers, and forced them back under the river-banks, but during the fight the *jefe politico* was killed. The Rangers were in a fair way to be overcome by the Mexicans, when Lieutenant Clendenin turned a Gatling loose from the American side and covered their position. A parley

---

* Mexican law of shooting escaped or resisting prisoners.

ensued, but McNally refused to go back without the cattle, which the Mexicans had finally to surrender.

At another time McNally received word through spies of an intended raid of Mexican cattle-thieves under the leadership of Cammelo Lerma. At Resaca de la Palma, McNally struck the depredators with but sixteen men. They had seventeen men and five hundred head of stolen cattle. In a running fight for miles McNally's men killed sixteen bandits, while only one escaped. A young Ranger by the name of Smith was shot dead by Cammelo Lerma as he dismounted to look at the dying bandit. The dead bodies were piled in ox-carts and dumped in the public square at Brownsville. McNally also captured King Fisher's band in an old log house in Dimmit County, but they were not convicted.

Showing the nature of Ranger work, an incident which occurred to my acquaintance, Captain Lea Hall, will illustrate. In De Witt County there was a feud. One dark night sixteen masked men took a sick man, one Dr. Brazel, and two of his boys, from their beds, and, despite the imploring mother and daughter, hanged the doctor and one son to a tree. The other boy escaped in the green corn. Nothing was done to punish the crime, as the lynchers were men of property and influence in the country. No man dared speak above his breath about the affair.

Captain Hall, by secret-service men, discovered the perpetrators, and also that they were to be gathered at a wedding on a certain night. He surrounded the house and demanded their surrender, at the same time saying that he did not want to kill the women and children. Word returned that they would kill him and all his Rangers. Hall told them to allow their women and children to depart, which was done; then, springing on the gallery of the house, he shouted, "Now, gentlemen, you can go to killing Rangers; but if you don't surrender, the Rangers will go to killing you." This was too frank a willingness for midnight assassins, and they gave up.

Spies had informed him that robbers intended sacking Campbell's store in Wolfe City. Hall and his men lay behind the counters to receive them on the designated night. They were allowed to enter, when Hall's men, rising, opened fire—the robbers replying. Smoke filled the room, which was fairly illuminated by the flashes of the guns— but the robbers were all killed, much to the disgust of the lawyers, no doubt, though I could never hear that honest people mourned.

The man Hall was himself a gentleman of the romantic Southern soldier type, and he entertained the highest ideals, with which it would be extremely unsafe to trifle, if I may judge. Captain Shely, our other visitor, was a herculean, black-eyed man, fairly fizzing with nervous energy. He is also exceedingly shrewd, as befits the greater concreteness of the modern Texas law, albeit he too has trailed bandits in the chaparral, and rushed in on their camp-fires at night, as two big bullet-holes in his skin will attest. He it was who arrested Polk, the defaulting treasurer of Tennessee. He rode a Spanish pony sixty-two miles in six hours, and arrested Polk, his guide, and two private detectives, whom Polk had bribed to set him over the Rio Grande.

When the land of Texas was bought up and fenced with wire, the old settlers who had used the land did not readily recognize the new régime. They raised the rallying-cry of "free grass and free water"—said they had fought the Indians off, and the land belonged to them. Taking nippers, they rode by night and cut down miles of fencing. Shely took the keys of a county jail from the frightened sheriff, made arrests by the score, and lodged them in the big new jail. The country-side rose in arms, surrounded the building, and threatened to tear it down. The big Ranger was not deterred by this outburst, but quietly went out into the mob, and with mock politeness delivered himself as follows:

" Do not tear down the jail, gentlemen—you have been taxed for years to build this fine structure—it is yours—do not tear it down. I will open the doors wide—you can all come in—do not tear down the jail; but there are twelve Rangers in there, with orders to kill as long as they can see. Come right in, gentlemen—but come fixed."

The mob was overcome by his civility.

Texas is to-day the only State in the Union where pistol-carrying is attended with great chances of arrest and fine. The law is supreme even in the lonely *jacails* out in the rolling waste of chaparral, and it was made so by the tireless riding, the deadly shooting, and the indomitable courage of the Texas Rangers.

THE BLUE QUAIL OF THE CACTUS

THE Quartermaster and I both had trouble which the doctors could not cure—it was January, and it would not do for us to sit in a " blind "; besides, I do not fancy that. There are ever so many men who are comfortable all over when they are sitting in a blind waiting on the vagrant flying of the ducks; but it is solemn, gloomy business, and, I must say, sufficient reason why they take a drink every fifteen minutes to keep up their enthusiasm. We both knew that the finest winter resort for shot-gun folks was in the Southwest—down on the Rio Grande in Texas—so we journeyed to Eagle Pass. As we got down from the train we saw Captain Febiger in his long military cloak by a lantern-light.

" Got any quail staked out for us, Feb?" asked the Quartermaster.

" Oodles," said Febiger; " get into my trap," and

we were rattled through the unlighted street out to the camp, and brought up by the Captain's quarters.

In the morning we unpacked our trunks, and had everything on the floor where we could see it, after the fashion with men. Captain Febiger's baby boy came in to help us rummage in the heaps of canvas clothes, ammunition, and what not besides, finally selecting for his amusement a loaded Colt's revolver and a freshly honed razor. We were terrorized by the possibilities of the combination. Our trying to take them away from the youngster only made him yell like a cavern of demons. We howled for his mother to come to our aid, which she finally did, and she separated the kid from his toys.

I put on my bloomers, when the Captain came in and viewed me, saying: " Texas bikes; but it doesn't bloom yet. I don't know just what Texas will do if you parade in those togs—but you can try."

As we sauntered down the dusty main street, Texas lounged in the doorways or stood up in its buggy and stared at me. Texas grinned cheerfully, too, but I did not care, so long as Texas kept its hand out of its hip pocket. I was content to help educate Texas as to personal comfort, at no matter what cost to myself. We passed into

LUNCHEON IN THE DESERT

Mexico over the Long Bridge to call on Señor Muños, who is the local czar, in hopes of getting permits to be let alone by his chaparral-rangers while we shot quail on their soil. In Mexico when the people observe an Americano they simply shrug their shoulders; so our bloomers attracted no more contempt than would an X-ray or a trolley-car. Señor Muños gave the permits, after much stately compliment and many subtle ways, which made us feel under a cloud of obligation.

The next morning an ambulance and escort-wagon drove up to the Captain's quarters, and we loaded ourselves in—shot-guns, ammunition, blankets, and the precious paper of Señor Muños; for, only the week before, the custom-house rangers had carefully escorted an American hunting-party a long distance back to the line for lack of the little paper and red seals. We rattled over the bridge, past the Mexican barrack, while its dark-skinned soldiery — who do not shoot quails — lounged in the sunshine against the whitewashed wall.

At the first outpost of the customs a little man, whose considerable equatorial proportions were girted with a gun, examined our paper, and waved us on our way. Under the railroad bridge of the International an engineer blew his whistle, and our mules climbed on top of each other in their terror.

We wound along the little river, through irrigating ditches, past dozens of those deliciously quaint adobe houses, past the inevitable church, past a dead pony, ran over a chicken, made the little seven-year-old girls take their five-year-old brothers up in their arms for protection, and finally we climbed a long hill. At the top stretched an endless plain. The road forked; presently it branched; anon it grew into twigs of white dust on the gray levels of the background. The local physician of Eagle Pass was of our party, and he was said to know where a certain tank was to be found, some thirty miles out in the desert, but no man yet created could know which twig of the road to take. He decided on one—changed his mind—got out of the ambulance, scratched his head, pondered, and finally resolution settled on his face. He motioned the driver to a certain twig, got in, and shut his mouth firmly, thus closing debate. We smoked silently, waiting for the doctor's mind to fog. He turned uneasily in his seat, like the agitated needle of a compass, and even in time hazarded the remark that something did not look natural; but there was nothing to look at but flat land and flat sky, unless a hawk sailing here and there. At noon we lunched at the tail of the ambulance, and gently "jollied" the doctor's topography. We pushed on. Later in the afternoon the thirsty

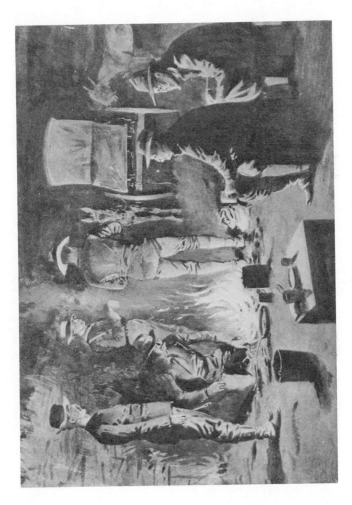

SUPPER IN THE CORRAL

mules went slowly. The doctor had by this time admitted his doubts—some long blue hills on the sky-line ought to be farther to the west, according to his remembrance. As no one else had any ideas on the subject, the doctor's position was not enviable. We changed our course, and travelled many weary miles through the chaparral, which was high enough to stop our vision, and stiff enough to bar our way, keeping us to narrow roads. At last the bisecting cattle trails began to converge, and we knew that they led to water— which they did ; for shortly we saw a little broken adobe, a tumbled brush corral, the plastered gate of an *acéquia*, and the blue water of the tank.

To give everything its due proportion at this point, we gathered to congratulate the doctor as we passed the flask. The camp was pitched within the corral, and while the cook got supper we stood in the after-glow on the bank of the tank and saw the ducks come home, heard the mud-hens squddle, while high in the air flew the long line of sand-hill cranes with a hoarse clangor. It was quite dark when we sat on the " grub " chests and ate by the firelight, while out in the desert the coyotes shrilled to the monotonous accompaniment of the mules crunching their feed and stamping wearily. To-morrow it was proposed to hunt ducks in their morning flight, which means getting up before daylight, so bed found us early. It seemed but a minute after I had sought my blankets when I was being abused by the Captain, being pushed with his foot—fairly rolled over by him—he even standing on my body as he shouted, " Get up, if you are going hunting. It will be light directly—get up !" And this, constantly recurring, is one reason why I do not care for duck-shooting.

But, in order to hunt, I had to get up, and file off in the line of ghosts, stumbling, catching on the chaparral, and splashing in the mud. I led a setter-dog, and was presently directed to sit down in some damp grass, because it was a good place— certainly not to sit down in, but for other reasons. I sat there in the dark, petting the good dog, and watching the sky grow pale in the east. This is not to mention the desire for breakfast, or the damp, or the sleepiness, but this is really the larger part of duck-hunting. Of course if I later had a dozen good shots it might compensate—but I did not have a dozen shots.

The day came slowly out of the east, the mud-hens out in the marsh splashed about in the rushes, a sailing hawk was visible against the gray sky overhead, and I felt rather insignificant, not to say contemptible, as I sat there in the loneliness of this big nature which worked around me. The dog dignified the situation—he was a part of

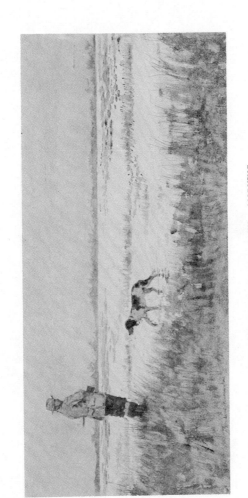

ON THE SHORE OF THE TANK — MORNING

nature's belongings—while I somehow did not seem to grace the solitude. The grays slowly grew into browns on the sedge-grass, and the water to silver. A bright flash of fire shot out of the dusk far up in the gloom, and the dull report of a shot-gun came over the tank. Black objects fled across the sky—the ducks were flying. I missed one or two, and grew weary—none came near enough to my lair. Presently it was light, and I got a fair shot. My bird tumbled into the rushes out in front of me, and the setter bounded in to retrieve. He searched vehemently, but the wounded duck dived in front of him. He came ashore shortly, and lying down, he bit at himself and pawed and rolled. He was a mass of cockle-burs. I took him on my lap and laboriously picked cockle-burs out of his hair for a half-hour; then, shouldering my gun, I turned tragically to the water and anathematized its ducks—all ducks, my fellow-duckers, all thoughts and motives concerning ducks—and then strode into the chaparral.

"Hie on! hie on!" I tossed my arm, and the setter began to hunt beautifully—glad, no doubt, to leave all thoughts of the cockle-burs and evasive ducks behind. I worked up the shore of the tank, keeping back in the brush, and got some fun. After chasing about for some time I came out near the water. My dog pointed. I glided forward, and came near shooting the Quartermaster, who sat in a bunch of sedge-grass, with a dead duck by his side. He was smoking, and was disgusted with ducks. He joined me, and shortly, as we crossed the road, the long Texas doctor, who owned the dog, came striding down the way. He was ready for quail now, and we started.

The quail-hunting is active work. The dog points, but one nearly always finds the birds running from one prickly-pear bush to another. They do not stand, rarely flush, and when they do get up it is only to swoop ahead to the nearest cover, where they settle quickly. One must be sharp in his shooting — he cannot select his distance, for the cactus lies thick about, and the little running bird is only on view for the shortest of moments. You must overrun a dog after his first point, since he works too close behind them. The covey will keep together if not pursued with too much haste, and one gets shot after shot; still, at last you must run lively, as the frightened covey scurry along at a remarkable pace. Heavy shot are necessary, since the blue quail carry lead like Marshal Masséna, and are much harder to kill than the bob-white. Three men working together can get shooting enough out of a bunch—the chase often continuing for a mile, when the covey gradually separate, the sportsmen following individual birds.

RUNNING BLUE QUAIL

THE BLUE QUAIL OF THE CACTUS

Where the prickly-pear cactus is thickest, there are the blue quail, since that is their feed and water supply. This same cactus makes a difficulty of pursuit, for it bristles with spines, which come off on your clothing, and when they enter the skin make most uncomfortable and persistent sores. The Quartermaster had an Indian tobacco-bag dangling at his belt, and as it flopped in his progress it gathered prickers, which it shortly transferred to his luckless legs, until he at last detected the reason why he bristled so fiercely. And the poor dog—at every covey we had to stop and pick needles out of him. The haunts of the blue quail are really no place for a dog, as he soon becomes useless. One does not need him, either, since the blue quail will not flush until actually kicked into the air.

Jack and cotton-tail rabbits fled by hundreds before us. They are everywhere, and afford good shooting between coveys, it being quick work to get a cotton-tail as he flashes between the net-work of protecting cactus. Coyotes lope away in our front, but they are too wild for a shot-gun. It must ever be in a man's mind to keep his direction, because it is such a vastly simple thing to get lost in the chaparral, where you cannot see a hundred yards. Mexico has such a considerable territory that a man on foot may find it inconvenient to beat up a town in the desolation of thorn-bush.

There is an action about blue-quail shooting which is next to buffalo shooting—it's run, shoot, pick up your bird, scramble on in your endeavor to keep the skirmish-line of your two comrades; and at last, when you have concluded to stop, you can mop your forehead—the Mexican sun shines hot even in midwinter.

Later in the afternoon we get among bob-white in a grassy tract, and while they are clean work—good dog-play, and altogether more satisfactory shooting than any other I know of—I am yet much inclined to the excitement of chasing after game which you can see at intervals. Let it not be supposed that it is less difficult to hit a running blue quail as he shoots through the brush than a flying bob-white, for the experience of our party has settled that, and one gets ten shots at the blue to one at the bob-white, because of their number. As to eating, we could not tell the difference; but I will not insist that this is final. A man who comes in from an all day's run in the brush does not care whether the cook gives him boiled beans, watermelon, or crackers and jam; so how is he to know what a bird's taste is when served to a tame appetite?

At intervals we ran into the wild cattle which

TOO BIG GAME FOR NUMBER SIX

threaded their way to water, and it makes one nervous. It is of no use to say "Soo-bossy," or to give him a charge of No. 6; neither is it well to run. If the *matadores* had any of the sensations which I have experienced, the gate receipts at the bull-rings would have to go up. When a big long-horn fastens a quail-shooter with his great open brown eye in a chaparral thicket, you are not inclined to "call his hand." If he will call it a misdeal, you are with him.

We were banging away, the Quartermaster and I, when a human voice began yelling like mad from the brush ahead. We advanced, to find a Mexican—rather well gotten up—who proceeded to wave his arms like a parson who had reached "sixthly" in his sermon, and who proceeded thereat to overwhelm us with his eloquence. The Quarter-master and I "*buenos dias-ed*" and "*si, señor-ed*" him in our helpless Spanish, and asked each other, nervously, "What de'll." After a long time he seemed to be getting through with his subject, his sentences became separated, he finally emitted monosyllables only along with his scowls, and we tramped off into the brush. It was a pity he spent so much energy, since it could only arouse our curiosity without satisfying it.

In camp that night we told the Captain of our excited Mexican friend out in the brush, and our cook had seen sinister men on ponies passing near our camp. The Captain became solicitous, and stationed a night-guard over his precious government mules. It would never do to have a bandit get away with a U. S. brand. It never does matter about private property, but anything with U. S. on it has got to be looked after, like a croupy child.

We had some good days' sport, and no more formidable enterprise against the night-guard was attempted than the noisy approach of a white jackass. The tents were struck and loaded when it began to rain. We stood in the shelter of the escort-wagon, and the storm rose to a hurricane. Our corral became a tank; but shortly the black clouds passed north, and we pulled out. The twig ran into a branch, and the branch struck the trunk near the bluffs over the Rio Grande, and in town there stood the Mexican soldiers leaning against the wall as we had left them. We wondered if they had moved meanwhile.

A SERGEANT OF THE OR-
PHAN TROOP

WHILE it is undisputed that Captain Dodd's troop of the Third Cavalry is not an orphan, and is, moreover, quite as far from it as any troop of cavalry in the world, all this occurred many years ago, when it was, at any rate, so called. There was nothing so very unfortunate about it, from what I can gather, since it seems to have fought well on its own hook, quite up to all expectations, if not beyond. No officer at that time seemed to care to connect his name with such a rioting, nose-breaking band of desperado cavalrymen, unless it was temporarily, and that was always in the field, and never in garrison. However, in this case it did not have even an officer in the field. But let me go on to my sergeant.

This one was a Southern gentleman, or rather a boy, when he refugeed out of Fredericksburg with his family, before the Federal advance, in a wagon belonging to a Mississippi rifle regiment; but nevertheless some years later he got to be a gentleman, and passed through the Virginia Military Institute with honor. The desire to be a soldier consumed him, but the vicissitudes of the times compelled him, if he wanted to be a soldier, to be a private one, which he became by duly enlisting in the Third Cavalry. He struck the Orphan Troop.

Physically, Nature had slobbered all over Carter Johnson; she had lavished on him her very last charm. His skin was pink, albeit the years of Arizona sun had heightened it to a dangerous red; his mustache was yellow and ideally military; while his pure Virginia accent, fired in terse and jerky form at friend and enemy alike, relieved his natural force of character by a shade of humor. He was thumped and bucked and pounded into what was in the seventies considered a proper frontier soldier, for in those days the nursery idea had not been lugged into the army. If a sergeant bade a soldier " go " or " do," he instantly " went " or "did"—otherwise the sergeant belted him over the head with his six-shooter, and had him taken off in a cart. On pay-days, too, when men who did not care to get drunk went to bed in barracks, they slept under their bunks and not in them, which was conducive to longevity and a good night's rest. When buffalo were scarce they ate the army rations in those wild days; they had a fight often enough to earn thirteen dollars, and at times a good deal more. This was the way with all men at that time, but it was rough on recruits.

So my friend Carter Johnson wore through some years, rose to be a corporal, finally a sergeant, and did many daring deeds. An atavism from "the old border riders" of Scotland shone through the boy, and he took on quickly. He could act the others off the stage and sing them out of the theatre in his chosen profession.

There was fighting all day long around Fort Robinson, Nebraska—a bushwhacking with Dull-Knife's band of the Northern Cheyennes, the Spartans of the plains. It was January; the snow lay deep on the ground, and the cold was knife-like as it thrust at the fingers and toes of the Orphan Troop. Sergeant Johnson with a squad of twenty men, after having been in the saddle all night, was in at the post drawing rations for the troop. As they were packing them up for transport, a detachment of F Troop came galloping by, led by the sergeant's friend, Corporal Thornton. They pulled up.

"Come on, Carter—go with us. I have just heard that some troops have got a bunch of Injuns corralled out in the hills. They can't get 'em

35

down. Let's go help 'em. It's a chance for the fight of your life. Come on."

Carter hesitated for a moment. He had drawn the rations for his troop, which was in sore need of them. It might mean a court-martial and the loss of his chevrons—but a fight! Carter struck his spurred heels, saying, "Come on, boys; get your horses; we will go."

The line of cavalry was half lost in the flying snow as it cantered away over the white flats. The dry powder crunched under the thudding hoofs, the carbines banged about, the overcoat capes blew and twisted in the rushing air, the horses grunted and threw up their heads as the spurs went into their bellies, while the men's faces were serious with the interest in store. Mile after mile rushed the little column, until it came to some bluffs, where it drew reign and stood gazing across the valley to the other hills.

Down in the bottoms they espied an officer and two men sitting quietly on their horses, and on riding up found a lieutenant gazing at the opposite bluffs through a glass. Far away behind the bluffs a sharp ear could detect the reports of guns.

"We have been fighting the Indians all day here," said the officer, putting down his glass and turning to the two "non-coms." "The command

"MILE AFTER MILE RUSHED THE LITTLE COLUMN"

has gone around the bluffs. I have just seen Indians up there on the rim-rocks. I have sent for troops, in the hope that we might get up there. Sergeant, deploy as skirmishers, and we will try."

At a gallop the men fanned out, then forward at a sharp trot across the flats, over the little hills, and into the scrub pine. The valley gradually narrowed until it forced the skirmishers into a solid body, when the lieutenant took the lead, with the command tailing out in single file. The signs of the Indians grew thicker and thicker—a skirmisher's nest here behind a scrub-pine bush, and there by the side of a rock. Kettles and robes lay about in the snow, with three "bucks" and some women and children sprawling about, frozen as they had died; but all was silent except the crunch of the snow and the low whispers of the men as they pointed to the telltales of the morning's battle.

As the column approached the precipitous rim-rock the officer halted, had the horses assembled in a side cañon, putting Corporal Thornton in charge. He ordered Sergeant Johnson to again advance his skirmish-line, in which formation the men moved forward, taking cover behind the pine scrub and rocks, until they came to an open space of about sixty paces, while above it towered the cliff for twenty feet in the sheer. There the

Indians had been last seen. The soldiers lay tight in the snow, and no man's valor impelled him on. To the casual glance the rim-rock was impassable. The men were discouraged and the officer nonplussed. A hundred rifles might be covering the rock fort for all they knew. On closer examination a cutting was found in the face of the rock which was a rude attempt at steps, doubtless made long ago by the Indians. Caught on a bush above, hanging down the steps, was a lariat, which, at the bottom, was twisted around the shoulders of a dead warrior. They had evidently tried to take him up while wounded, but he had died and had been abandoned.

After cogitating, the officer concluded not to order his men forward, but he himself stepped boldly out into the open and climbed up. Sergeant Johnson immediately followed, while an old Swedish soldier by the name of Otto Bordeson fell in behind them. They walked briskly up the hill, and placing their backs against the wall of rock, stood gazing at the Indian.

With a grin the officer directed the men to advance. The sergeant, seeing that he realized their serious predicament, said:

" I think, lieutenant, you had better leave them where they are; we are holding this rock up pretty hard."

38

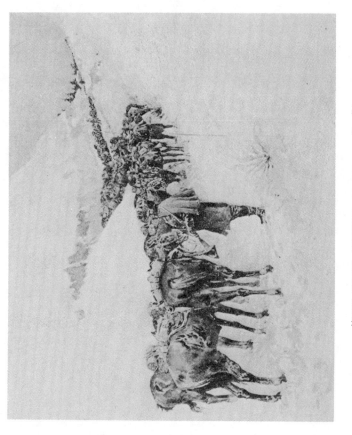

"THE HORSES ASSEMBLED IN A SIDE CAÑON"

They stood there and looked at each other. "We's in a fix," said Otto.

"I want volunteers to climb this rock," finally demanded the officer.

The sergeant looked up the steps, pulled at the lariat, and commented: "Only one man can go at a time; if there are Indians up there, an old squaw can kill this command with a hatchet; and if there are no Indians, we can all go up."

The impatient officer started up, but the sergeant grabbed him by the belt. He turned, saying, "If I haven't got men to go, I will climb myself."

"Stop, lieutenant. It wouldn't look right for the officer to go. I have noticed a pine-tree, the branches of which spread over the top of the rock," and the sergeant pointed to it. "If you will make the men cover the top of the rim-rock with their rifles, Bordeson and I will go up;" and turning to the Swede, "Will you go, Otto?"

"I will go anywhere the sergeant does," came his gallant reply.

"Take your choice, then, of the steps or the pine - tree," continued the Virginian; and after a rather short but sharp calculation the Swede declared for the tree, although both were death if the Indians were on the rim-rock. He immediately began sidling along the rock to the tree, and slowly commenced the ascent. The sergeant took a few steps up the cutting, holding on by the rope. The officer stood out and smiled quizzically. Jeers came from behind the soldiers' bushes —" Go it, Otto! Go it, Johnson! Your feet are loaded! If a snow-bird flies, you will drop dead! Do you need any help? You'd make a hell of a sailor!" and other gibes.

The gray clouds stretched away monotonously over the waste of snow, and it was cold. The two men climbed slowly, anon stopping to look at each other and smile. They were monkeying with death.

At last the sergeant drew himself up, slowly raised his head, and saw snow and broken rock. Otto lifted himself likewise, and he too saw nothing Rifle-shots came clearly to their ears from far in front—many at one time, and scattering at others. Now the soldiers came briskly forward, dragging up the cliff in single file. The dull noises of the fight came through the wilderness. The skirmish-line drew quickly forward and passed into the pine woods, but the Indian trails scattered. Dividing into sets of four, they followed on the tracks of small parties, wandering on until night threatened. At length the main trail of the fugitive band ran across their front, bringing the command together. It was too late for the officer to

"THE TWO MEN CLIMBED SLOWLY"

get his horses before dark, nor could he follow with his exhausted men, so he turned to the sergeant and asked him to pick some men and follow on the trail. The sergeant picked Otto Bordeson, who still affirmed that he would go anywhere that Johnson went, and they started. They were old hunting companions, having confidence in each other's sense and shooting. They ploughed through the snow, deeper and deeper into the pines, then on down a cañon where the light was failing. The sergeant was sweating freely; he raised his hand to press his fur cap backward from his forehead. He drew it quickly away; he stopped and started, caught Otto by the sleeve, and drew a long breath. Still holding his companion, he put his glove again to his nose, sniffed at it again, and with a mighty tug brought the startled Swede to his knees, whispering, " I smell Indians; I can sure smell 'em, Otto—can you ? "

Otto sniffed, and whispered back, " Yes, plain ! "

" We are ambushed ! Drop ! " and the two soldiers sunk in the snow. A few feet in front of them lay a dark thing; crawling to it, they found a large calico rag, covered with blood.

" Let's do something, Carter; we's in a fix."

" If we go down, Otto, we are gone; if we go back, we are gone; let's go forward," hissed the sergeant.

Slowly they crawled from tree to tree.

" Don't you see the Injuns ?" said the Swede, as he pointed to the rocks in front, where lay their dark forms. The still air gave no sound. The cathedral of nature, with its dark pine trunks starting from gray snow to support gray sky, was dead. Only human hearts raged, for the forms which held them lay like black bowlders.

" Egah—lelah washatah," yelled the sergeant.

Two rifle-shots rang and reverberated down the cañon ; two more replied instantly from the soldiers. One Indian sunk, and his carbine went clanging down the rocks, burying itself in the snow. Another warrior rose slightly, took aim, but Johnson's six-shooter cracked again, and the Indian settled slowly down without firing. A squaw moved slowly in the half-light to where the buck lay. Bordeson drew a bead with his carbine.

"Don't shoot the woman, Otto. Keep that hole covered ; the place is alive with Indians ;" and both lay still.

A buck rose quickly, looked at the sergeant, and dropped back. The latter could see that he had him located, for he slowly poked his rifle up without showing his head. Johnson rolled swiftly to one side, aiming with his deadly revolver. Up popped the Indian's head, crack went the six-shooter; the head turned slowly, leaving the top exposed. Crack again went the alert gun of the soldier, the ball striking the head just below the scalp-lock and instantly jerking the body into a kneeling position.

Then all was quiet in the gloomy woods.

After a time the sergeant addressed his voice to the lonely place in Sioux, telling the women to come out and surrender—to leave the bucks, etc.

An old squaw rose sharply to her feet, slapped her breast, shouted "Lelah washatah," and gathering up a little girl and a bundle, she strode forward to the soldiers. Three other women followed, two of them in the same blanket.

"Are there any more bucks?" roared the sergeant, in Sioux.

"No more alive," said the old squaw, in the same tongue.

"Keep your rifle on the hole between the rocks; watch these people; I will go up," directed the sergeant, as he slowly mounted to the ledge, and with levelled six-shooter peered slowly over. He stepped in and stood looking down on the dead warriors.

A yelling in broken English smote the startled sergeant. "Tro up your hands, you d—— Injun! I'll blow the top off you!" came through the quiet. The sergeant sprang down to see the

43

Swede standing with carbine levelled at a young buck confronting him with a drawn knife in his hands, while his blanket lay back on the snow.

" He's a buck—he ain't no squaw; he tried to creep on me with a knife. I'm going to kill him," shouted the excited Bordeson.

" No, no, don't kill him. Otto, don't you kill him," expostulated Johnson, as the Swede's finger clutched nervously at the trigger, and turning, he roared, " Throw away that knife, you d—— Indian !"

The detachment now came charging in through the snow, and gathered around excitedly. A late arrival came up, breathing heavily, dropped his gun, and springing up and down, yelled, " Be jabbers, I have got among om at last !" A general laugh went up, and the circle of men broke into a straggling line for the return. The sergeant took the little girl up in his arms. She grabbed him fiercely by the throat like a wild-cat, screaming. While nearly choking, he yet tried to mollify her, while her mother, seeing no harm was intended, pacified her in the soft gutturals of the race. She relaxed her grip, and the brave Virginian packed her down the mountain, wrapped in his soldier cloak. The horses were reached in time, and the prisoners put on double behind the soldiers, who fed them crackers as they marched. At

"'THE BRAVE CHEYENNES WERE RUNNING THROUGH THE FROSTY HILLS"

two o'clock in the morning the little command rode
into Fort Robinson and dismounted at the guard-
house. The little girl, who was asleep and half
frozen in Johnson's overcoat, would not go to her
mother: poor little cat, she had found a nest.
The sergeant took her into the guard - house,
where it was warm. She soon fell asleep, and
slowly he undid her, delivering her to her mother.

On the following morning he came early to the
guard-house, loaded with trifles for his little Indian
girl. He had expended all his credit at the post-
trader's, but he could carry sentiment no further,
for " To horse!" was sounding, and he joined the
Orphan Troop to again ride on the Dull-Knife
trail. The brave Cheyennes were running through
the frosty hills, and the cavalry horses pressed
hotly after. For ten days the troops surrounded
the Indians by day, and stood guard in the snow
by night, but coming day found the ghostly warriors gone and their rifle-pits empty. They were
cut off and slaughtered daily, but the gallant warriors were fighting to their last nerve. Towards
the end they were cooped in a gully on War-Bon-
natt Creek, where they fortified; but two six-
pounders had been hauled out, and were turned
on their works. The four troops of cavalry stood
to horse on the plains all day, waiting for the poor
wretches to come out, while the guns roared,

45

ploughing the frozen dirt and snow over their little stronghold; but they did not come out. It was known that all the provisions they had was the dead horse of a corporal of E Troop, which had been shot within twenty paces of their rifle-pits.

So, too, the soldiers were starving, and the poor Orphans had only crackers to eat. They were freezing also, and murmuring to be led to "the charge," that they might end it there, but they were an orphan troop, and must wait for others to say. The sergeant even asked an officer to let them go, but was peremptorily told to get back in the ranks.

The guns ceased at night, while the troops drew off to build fires, warm their rigid fingers, thaw out their buffalo moccasins, and munch crackers, leaving a strong guard around the Cheyennes. In the night there was a shooting—the Indians had charged through and had gone.

The day following they were again surrounded on some bluffs, and the battle waged until night. Next day there was a weak fire from the Indian position on the impregnable bluffs, and presently it ceased entirely. The place was approached with care and trepidation, but was empty. Two Indian boys, with their feet frozen, had been left as decoys, and after standing off four troops of

"THROUGH THE SMOKE SPRANG THE DARING SOLDIER"

cavalry for hours, they too had in some mysterious way departed.

But the pursuit was relentless ; on, on over the rolling hills swept the famishing troopers, and again the Spartan band turned at bay, firmly intrenched on a bluff as before. This was the last stand—nature was exhausted. The soldiers surrounded them, and Major Wessells turned the handle of the human vise. The command gathered closer about the doomed pits—they crawled on their bellies from one stack of sage-brush to the next. They were freezing. The order to charge came to the Orphan Troop, and yelling his command, Sergeant Johnson ran forward. Up from the sage-brush floundered the stiffened troopers, following on. They ran over three Indians, who lay sheltered in a little cut, and these killed three soldiers together with an old frontier sergeant who wore long hair, but they were destroyed in turn. While the Orphans swarmed under the hill, a rattling discharge poured from the rifle-pits ; but the troop had gotten under the fire, and it all passed over their heads. On they pressed, their blood now quickened by excitement, crawling up the steep, while volley on volley poured over them. Within nine feet of the pits was a rim-rock ledge over which the Indian bullets swept, and here the charge was stopped. It now became a duel.

Every time a head showed on either side, it drew fire like a flue-hole. Suddenly our Virginian sprang on the ledge, and like a trill on a piano poured a six-shooter into the intrenchment, and dropped back.

Major Wessells, who was commanding the whole force, crawled to the position of the Orphan Troop, saying, "Doing fine work, boys. Sergeant, I would advise you to take off that red scarf"—when a bullet cut the major across the breast, whirling him around and throwing him. A soldier, one Lannon, sprang to him and pulled him down the bluff, the major protesting that he was not wounded, which proved to be true, the bullet having passed through his heavy clothes.

The troops had drawn up on the other sides, and a perfect storm of bullets whirled over the intrenchments. The powder blackened the faces of the men, and they took off their caps or had them shot off. To raise the head for more than a fraction of a second meant death.

Johnson had exchanged five shots with a fine-looking Cheyenne, and every time he raised his eye to a level with the rock White Antelope's gun winked at him.

"You will get killed directly," yelled Lannon to Johnson; "they have you spotted."

The smoke blew and eddied over them; again

"THIS TIME THE AIR GREW CLEAR"

Johnson rose, and again White Antelope's pistol cracked an accompaniment to his own; but with movement like lightning the sergeant sprang through the smoke, and fairly shoving his carbine to White Antelope's breast, he pulled the trigger. A 50-calibre gun boomed in Johnson's face, and a volley roared from the pits, but he fell backward into cover. His comrades set him up to see if any red stains came through the grime, but he was unhurt.

The firing grew; a blue haze hung over the hill. Johnson again looked across the glacis, but again his eye met the savage glare of White Antelope.

"I haven't got him yet, Lannon, but I will;" and Sergeant Johnson again slowly reloaded his pistol and carbine.

"Now, men, give them a volley!" ordered the enraged man, and as volley answered volley, through the smoke sprang the daring soldier, and standing over White Antelope as the smoke swirled and almost hid him, he poured his six balls into his enemy, and thus died one brave man at the hands of another in fair battle. The sergeant leaped back and lay down among the men, stunned by the concussions. He said he would do no more. His mercurial temperament had undergone a change, or, to put it better, he conceived it to be outrageous to fight these poor people, five against one. He characterized it as " a d—— infantry fight," and rising, talked in Sioux to the enemy—asked them to surrender, or they must otherwise die. A young girl answered him, and said they would like to. An old woman sprang on her and cut her throat with a dull knife, yelling meanwhile to the soldiers that " they would never surrender alive," and saying what she had done.

Many soldiers were being killed, and the fire from the pits grew weaker. The men were beside themselves with rage. " Charge !" rang through the now still air from some strong voice, and, with a volley, over the works poured the troops, with six-shooters going, and clubbed carbines. Yells, explosions, and amid a whirlwind of smoke the soldiers and Indians swayed about, now more slowly and quieter, until the smoke eddied away. Men stood still, peering about with wild open eyes through blackened faces. They held desperately to their weapons. An old bunch of buckskin rags rose slowly and fired a carbine aimlessly. Twenty bullets rolled and tumbled it along the ground, and again the smoke drifted off the mount. This time the air grew clear. Buffalo-robes lay all about, blood spotted everywhere. The dead bodies of thirty-two Cheyennes lay, writhed and twisted, on the packed snow, and among them many women and children, cut and furrowed with lead. In a corner was a pile of wounded squaws, half covered with dirt swept over them by the storm of bullets. One broken creature half raised herself from the bunch. A maddened trumpeter threw up his gun to shoot, but Sergeant Johnson leaped and kicked his gun out of his hands high into the air, saying, "This fight is over."

THE SPIRIT OF MAHONGUI

It is so I have called this old document, which is an extract from the memoirs of le Chevalier Bailloquet, a Frenchman living in Canada, where he was engaged in the Indian fur trade, about the middle of the seventeenth century, and as yet they are unpublished.

It is written in English, since the author lived his latter life in England, having left Canada as the result of troubles with the authorities.

He was captured by the Iroquois, and after living with them some time, made his escape to the Dutch.

My Chevalier rambles somewhat, although I have been at pains to cut out extraneous matter. It is also true that many will not believe him in these days, for out of their puny volition they will analyze, and out of their discontent they will scoff. But to those I say, Go to your microbes, your statistics, your volts, and your bicycles, and leave me the truth of other days.

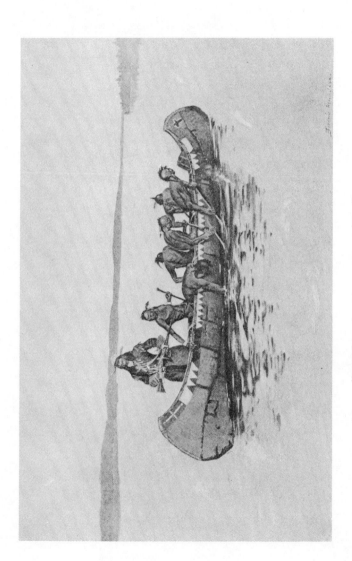

"THIS WAS A FATAL EMBARQUATION"

The Chevalier was on a voyage from Quebec to Montreal; let him begin:

The next day we embarqued, though not w^{th}out confufion, becaufe many weare not content, nor fatiffied. What a pleafure ye two fathers to fee them trott up and downe ye rocks to gett their manage into ye boat. The boats weare fo loaded that many could not proceed if foul weather fhould happen. I could not perfuade myfelf to ftay wth this concourfe as ye weather was faire for my journie. W^{th}out adoe, I gott my fix wild men to paddle on ye way.

This was a fatal embarquation, butt I did not miftruft that ye Iriquoits weare abroad in ye foreft, for I had been at ye Peace. Neverthelefs I find that thefe wild men doe naught butt what they refolve out of their bloodie mindednefs. We paffed the Point going out of ye Lake St. Peter, when ye Barbars appeared on ye watter-fide difcharging their mufkets at us, and embarquing for our purfuit.

"Kohe—kohe!"—came nearer ye fearfome warre cry of ye Iriquoit, making ye hearts of ye poore Hurron & ffrench alike to turn to water in their breafts. 2 of my favages weare ftrook downe at ye firft difcharge & another had his paddle cutt in twain, befides fhott holes through wch the watter poured apace. Thus weare we diminifhed and could not draw off.

The Barbars weare daubed wth paint, wch is ye figne of warre. They coming againft our boat ftruck downe our Hurrons wth hattchetts, fuch as did not jump into the watter, where alfo they weare in no wife faved.

But in my boat was a Hurron Captayne, who all his

life-time had killed many Iriquoits & by his name for vallor had come to be a great Captayne att home and abroad. We weare refolved fome execution & wth our gunns dealt a difcharge & drew our cutlaffes to ftrike ye foe. They environed us as we weare finking, and one fpake faying—"Brothers, cheere up and affure yourfelfe you fhall not be killed; thou art both men and Captaynes, as I myfelf am, and I will die in thy defenfe." And ye afforefaid crew fhewed fuch a horrid noise, of a sudden ye Iriquoit Captayne took hold about me— "Thou fhalt not die by another hand than mine."

Ye favages layd bye our armes & tyed us faft in a boat, one in one boat and one in another. We proceeded up ye river, rather fleeping than awake, for I thought never to efcape.

Att near funfett we weare taken on ye fhore, where ye wild men encamped bye making cottages of rind from off ye trees. They tyed ye Hurron Captayne to a trunk, he refolving moft bravely but deffparred to me, and I too deffparred. Neverthelefs he fang his fatal fong though ye fire made him as one wth the ague. They tooke out his heart and cut off fome of ye flefh of ye miferable, boyled it and eat it. This they wifhed not to doe att this time, but that ye Hurron had been fhott wth a ball under his girdle where it was not feen, though he would have died of his defperate wound. That was the miferable end of that wretch.

Whilft they weare bufy wth ye Hurron, they having ftripped me naked, tyed me above ye elbows, and wrought a rope about my middle. They afked me feveral queftions, I not being able to anfwer, they gave me great blows wth their fifts, then pulled out one of

54

my nails. Having loft all hopes, I refolved altogether to die, itt being folly to think otherwife.

I could not flee, butt was flung into a boat att daylight. Ye boats went all abreaft, ye wild men finging fome of their fatal fongs, others their howls of victory, ye wild " Kohes," beating giens & parchments, blowing whiftles, and all manner of tumult.

Thus did we proceed wth these ravening wolves, God having delivered a Chriftian into ye power of Satan.

I was nott ye only one in ye claws of thefe wolves, for we fell in wth 150 more of thefe cruels, who had Hurron captyves to ye number of 33 victims, wth heads alfoe ftuck on poles, of those who in God's mercie weare gone from their miferies. As for me, I was put in a boat wth one who had his fingers cutt & bourned. I afked him why ye Iriquoits had broak ye Peace, and he faid they had told him ye ffrench had broak ye Peace ; that ye ffrench had fet their pack of doggs on an olde Iriquoit woman who was eat up alive & that ye Iriquoits had told ye Hurron wild men that they had killed ye doggs, alfoe Hurrons and ffrench, faying that as to ye captyves, they would boyl doggs, Hurrons, and ffrench in ye fame kettle.

A great rain arofe, ye Iriquoits going to ye watter-fide did cover themfelvs wth their boats, holding ye cap-tyves ye meanwhile bye ropes bound about our ancles, while we ftood out in ye ftorm, wch was near to caufing me death from my nakednefs. When ye rain had abated, we purfued our way killing ftaggs, & I was given fome entrails, wch before I had only a little parched corne to ye extent of my handfull.

At a point we mett a gang of ye head hunters all on

ye fhore, dancing about a tree to wch was tyed a fine
ffrench maftiff dogg, wch was ftanding on its hinder
leggs, being lafhed up againft a tree by its middle. Ye
dogg was in a great terror, and frantic in its bonds. I
knew him for a dogg from ye fort att Mont-royal, kept
for to give warnings of ye Enemy's approach. It was a
ftrange fight for to fee ye Heathen rage about ye noble
dogg, but he itt was neverthelefs wch brought ye Barbars
againft us. He was only gott wth great difficulty, having killed one Barbar, and near to ferving others like-
wife.

They untyed ye dogg, I holding him one fide, and ye
other, wth cords they brought and tyed him in ye bow
of a boat wth 6 warriors to paddle him. Ye dogg boat
was ye Head, while ye reft came on up ye river finging
fatal fongs, triumph fongs, piping, howling, & ye dogg
above all wth his great noife. Ye Barbars weare more
delighted att ye captyve dogg than att all of us poore
Chriftians, for that they did fay he was no dogg. Ye
doggs wch ye wild men have are nott fo great as wolves,
they being little elfe & fmall att that. Ye maftiff was
confidered as a confequence to be a great intereft. This
one had near defeated their troupe & now was to be
horridly killed after ye bloody way of ye wild men.

Att camp they weare fleep moft of ye night, they
being aweary wth ye torture of ye Hurron Captayne
previoufly. Ye dogg was tyed & layd nott far off from
where I was alfoe tyed, butt over him weare 2 olde men,
who guarded him of a fear he would eat away his ropes.
Thefe men weare Elders or Priefts, fuch as are efteemed
for their power over fpirits, & they did keep up their
devil's fong ye night thro.

I made a vertue of neceffity & did fleep, butt was early caft into a boat to go on towards ye Enemy's countrie, tho we had raw meat given us, wth blows on ye mouth to make us ye more quickly devour itt. An Iriquoit who was the Captayne in our boat, bade me to be of a good courage, as they would not hurt me. Ye fmall knowledge I had of their fpeech made a better hope, butt one who could have underftood them would have been certainly in a great terror.

Thus we journied 8 days on ye Lake Champlaine, where ye wind and waves did fore befet our endeavors att times. As for meate we wanted none, as we had a ftore of ftaggs along ye watter-fide. We killed fome every day, more for fport than for need. We finding them on Ifles, made them go into ye watter, & after we killed above a fcore, we clipped ye ears of ye reft & hung bells on them, and then lett them loofe. What a fport to fee ye reft flye from them that had ye bells!

There came out of ye vaft foreft a multitude of bears, 300 at leaft together, making a horrid noife, breaking ye fmall trees. We fhott att them, butt they ftirred not a ftep. We weare much frightened that they ftirred nott att our fhooting. Ye great ffrench dogg would fain encounter them notwithftanding he was tyed. He made ye watter-fide to ring wth his heavy voife & from his eyes came flames of fyre & clouds from out his mouth. The bears did ftraightway flye wch much cheered ye Iriquoits. One faid to me they weare refolved nott to murder ye dogg, wch was a ftone-God in ye dogg fhape, or a witch, butt I could nott fully underftand. Ye wild men faid they had never heard their fathers fpeak of fo many bears.

When we putt ye kettle on, ye wild man who had captured me, gave me of meate to eat, & told me a ftory. " Brother," fays he, " itt is a thing to be admired to goe afar to travell. You muft know that tho I am olde, I have always loved ye ffrench for their goodnefs, but they fhould have given us to kill ye Algonkins. We fhould not warre againft ye ffrench, butt trade wth them for Caftors, who are better for traffic than ye Dutch. I was once a Captayne of 13 men againft ye Altignaonanton & ye ffrench. We ftayed 3 whole winters among ye Ennemy, butt in ye daytime durft not marche nor ftay out of ye deep foreft. We killed many, butt there weare devils who took my fon up in ye air fo I could never again get him back. Thefe devils weare as bigg as horriniacs,* & ye little blue birds wch attend upon them, faid itt was time for us to go back to our people, wch being refolved to do, we came back, butt nott of a fear of ye Ennemy. Our warre fong grew ftill on our lipps, as ye fnow falling in ye foreft. I have nott any more warred to the North, until I was told by ye fpirits to go to ye ffrench & recover my fon. My friend, I have dreamed you weare my fon ;" and henceforth I was not hurted nor ftarved for food.

We proceeded thro rivers & lakes & thro forefts where I was made to fupport burdens. When we weare come to ye village of ye Iriquoits we lay in ye woods becaufe that they would nott go into ye village in ye night time.

The following day we weare marched into ye brought† of ye Iriquoits. When we came in fight we heard noth-

* Moose.   † Borough.

58

THE OMEN OF THE LITTLE BLUE BIRDS

ing butt outcryes from one fide, as from ye other. Then came a mighty hoft of people & payd great heed to ye ffrench dogg, wch was ledd bye 2 men while round-about his neck was a girdle of porcelaine. They tormented ye poore Hurrons wth violence, butt about me was hung a long piece of porcelaine—ye girdle of my captor, & he ftood againft me. In ye meanwhile, many of ye village came about us, among wch a goode olde woman & a boy wth a hattchett came neere me. Ye olde woman covered me, & ye boy took me by my hand and led mee out of ye companie. What comforted me was that I had efcaped ye blowes. They brought me into ye village where ye olde woman fhowed me kindnefs. She took me into her cottage, & gave me to eat, butt my great terror took my ftumack away from me. I had ftayed an hour when a great companie came to fee me, of olde men wth pipes in their mouths. For a time they fat about, when they did lead me to another cabbin, w^{re} they fmoked & made me apprehend they fhould throw me into ye fyre. Butt itt proved otherwife, for ye olde woman followed me, fpeaking aloud, whome they anfwered wth a loud *ho,* then fhee tooke her girdle, and about me fhe tyed itt, fo brought me to her cottage & made me to fitt downe.

Then fhe gott me Indian corne toafted, & took away ye paint ye fellows had ftuck to my face. A maide greafed & combed my haire, & ye olde woman danced and fung, while my father bourned tobacco on a ftone. They gave me a blew coverlitt, ftockings, and fhoes. I layed wth her fon & did w^t I could to get familiarity wth them, and I fuffered no wrong, yet I was in a terror, for ye fatal fongs came from ye poore Hurrons. Ye olde

man inquired whether I was Afferony, a ffrench. I
affured him no, faying I was Panugaga, that is of their
nation, for wch he was pleafed.

My father feafted 200 men. My fifters made me clean
for that purpofe, and greafed my haire. They tyed me
wth 2 necklaces of porcelaine & garters of ye fame. My
father gave me a hattchett in my hand.

My father made a fpeech, fhowing many demonftra-
tions of vallor, broak a kettle of cagamite wth a hattchett.
So they fung, as is their ufual cuftom. Ye banquette
being over, all cryed to me " Shagon, Orimha "—that is
" be hearty!" Every one withdrew to his quarters.

Here follows a long account of his daily life
among the Indians, his hunting and observations,
which our space forbids. He had become meanwhile more familiar with the language. He goes on:

My father came into ye cabbin from ye grand caftle
& he fat him downe to fmoke. He faid ye Elders had
approved after much debate, & that ye ffrench dogg was
not a witch, but ye great warrior Mahongui, gone before,
whofe fpirit had rofe up into ye ffrench dogg & had
fpyed ye ffrench. Att ye council even foe ye dogg had
walked into ye centre of ye great cabbin, there faying
loudly to ye Elders what he was & that he muft be heard.
His voice muft be obeyed. His was not ye mocking
cryes of a witch from under an olde fnake-fkin, butt a
chief come from Paradife to comfort his own people.
My father afked me if I was agreed. I faid that witches
did not battile as openly as ye dogg, butt doe their evil
in ye dark.

"YE SPIRIT DOGG STRODE FROM YE DARKNESS & SAID IT WAS TIME"

Thefe wild men are fore befet wth witches and devils —more than Chriftians, as they deferve to be, for they are of Satan's own belonging.

My father dreamed att night, & fang about itt, making ye fire to bourne in our cabbin. We fatt to liften. He had mett ye ffrench dogg in ye foreft path bye night— he ftanding accrofs his way, & ye foreft was light from ye dogg's eyes, who fpake to my father faying, " I belong to ye dead folks—my hattchett is ruft—my bow is mould —I can no longer battile wth our Ennemy, butt I hover over you in warre—I direct your arrows to their breafts —I fmoothe ye little dry fticks & wett ye leaves under ye fhoes—I draw ye morning mift accrofs to fhield you —I carry ye ' Kohes' back and fore to bring your terror —I fling afide ye foeman's bulletts—go back and be ftrong in council."

My father even in ye night drew ye Elders in ye grand cabbin. He faid what he had feen and heard. Even then the great ffrench dogg gott from ye darknefs of ye cabbin, & ftrode into ye fyre. He roared enough to blow downe caftles in his might & they knew he was faying what he had told unto my father.

A great Captayne fent another night, & had ye Elders for to gather at ye grande cabbin. He had been pad- dling his boat upon ye river when ye dogg of Mahongui had walked out on ye watter thro ye mift. He was taller than ye foreft. So he fpake, faying " Mahongui fays—go tell ye people of ye Panugaga, itt is time for warre—ye corne is gathered—ye deer has changed his coat—there are no more Hurrons for me to eat. What is a Panugaga village wth no captyves ? Ye young men will talk as women doe, & ye Elders will grow content to watch a snow-bird hopp. Mahongui says itt is time."

Again att ye council fyre ye spirit dogg strode from ye darknes & said itt was time. Ye tobacco was bourned by ye Priests. In ye smoke ye Elders beheld ye Spirit of Mahongui. "Panugaga—Warre."

Soe my father saw ye ghost of ye departed one. He smoked long bye our cabbin fyre. He sang his battile song. I asked him to goe myself, even wth a hattchett, as I too was Panugaga. Butt he would in no wise listen. "You are nott meet," he says, "you sayest that your God is above. How will you make me believe that he is as goode as your black coats say? They doe lie & you see ye contrary; ffor first of all, ye Sun bournes us often, ye rain wetts us, ye winde makes us have shipwrake, ye thunder, ye lightening bournes & kills us, & all comes from above, & you say that itt is goode to be there. For my part, I will nott goe there. Contrary they say that ye reprobates & guilty goeth downe & bourne. They are mistaken; all is goode heare. Do nott you see that itt is ye Earthe that nourishes all living creatures—ye watter, ye fishes, & ye yus, and that corne & all other fruits come up, & that all things are nott soe contrary to us as that from above? Ye devils live in ye air & they took my son. When you see that ye Earthe is our Mother, then you will see that all things on itt are goode. Ye Earthe was made for ye Panugaga, & ye souls of our warriors help us against our Ennemy. Ye ffrench dogg is Mahongui's spirit. He tells us to goe to warre against ye ffrench. Would a ffrench dogg doe that? You are nott yett Panugaga to follow your father in warre."

THE ESSENTIALS AT FORT
ADOBE

THE Indian suns himself before the door of his tepee, dreaming of the past. For a long time now he has eaten of the white man's lotos—the bi-monthly beef-issue. I looked on him and won-dered at the new things. The buffalo, the war-path, all are gone. What of the cavalrymen over at Adobe—his Nemesis in the stirring days—are they, too, lounging in barracks, since his lordship no longer leads them trooping over the burning flats by day and through the ragged hills by night? I will go and see.

The blistered faces of men, the gaunt horses dragging stiffly along to the cruel spurring, the dirty lack-lustre of campaigning—that, of course, is no more. Will it be parades, and those soul-deadening "fours right" and "column left" affairs? Oh, my dear, let us hope not.

Nothing is so necessary in the manufacture of

soldiers, sure enough, but it is not hard to learn, and once a soldier knows it I can never understand why it should be drilled into him until it hurts. Besides, from another point of view, soldiers in rows and in lines do not compose well in pictures. I always feel, after seeing infantry drill in an armory, like Kipling's light-house keeper, who went insane looking at the cracks between the boards—they were all so horribly alike.

Then Adobe is away out West in the blistering dust, with no towns of any importance near it. I can understand why men might become listless when they are at field-work, with the full knowledge that nothing but their brothers are looking at them save the hawks and coyotes. It is different from Meyer, with its traps full of Congressmen and girls, both of whom are much on the minds of cavalrymen.

In due course I was bedded down at Adobe by my old friend the Captain, and then lay thinking of this cavalry business. It is a subject which thought does not simplify, but, like other great things, makes it complicate and recede from its votaries. To know essential details from unessential details is the study in all arts. Details there must be; they are the small things that make the big things. To apply this general order of things to this arm of the service kept me awake. There

is first the riding—simple enough if they catch
you young. There are bits, saddles, and cavalry
packs. I know men who have not spoken to each
other in years because they disagree about these.
There are the sore backs and colics — that is a
profession in itself. There are judgment of pace,
the battle tactics, the use of three very different
weapons; there is a world of history in this, in
forty languages. Then an ever-varying *terrain*
tops all. There are other things not confined to
cavalry, but regarded by all soldiers. The crown-
ing peculiarity of cavalry is the rapidity of its
movement, whereby a commander can lose the
carefully built up reputation of years in about the
time it takes a school-boy to eat a marsh-mallow.
After all, it is surely a hard profession — a very
blind trail to fame. I am glad I am not a cavalry-
man; still, it is the happiest kind of fun to look on
when you are not responsible; but it needs some
cultivation to understand and appreciate.

I remember a dear friend who had a taste for
out-of-doors. He penetrated deeply into the inte-
rior not long since to see these same troopers do
a line of heroics, with a band of Bannocks to support the rôle. The Indians could not finally be
got on the centre of the stage, but made hot-foot
for the agency. My friend could not see any good
in all this, nor was he satisfied with the first act

even. He must needs have a climax, and that not forthcoming, he loaded his disgust into a trunk line and brought it back to his club corner here in New York. He there narrated the failure of his first night; said the soldiers were not even dusty as advertised; damned the Indians keenly, and swore at the West by all his gods.

There was a time when I, too, regarded not the sketches in this art, but yearned for the finished product. That, however, is not exhibited generally over once in a generation.

At Adobe there are only eight troops — not enough to make a German nurse-girl turn her head in the street, and my friend from New York, with his Napoleonic largeness, would scoff out loud. But he and the nurse do not understand the significance; they have not the eyes to see. A starboard or a port horseshoe would be all one to them, and a crease in the saddle-blanket the smallest thing in the world, yet it might spoil a horse.

When the trumpets went in the morning I was sorry I had thought at all. It was not light yet, and I clung to my pillow. Already this cavalry has too much energy for my taste.

" If you want to see anything, you want to lead out," said the Captain, as he pounded me with a boot.

66

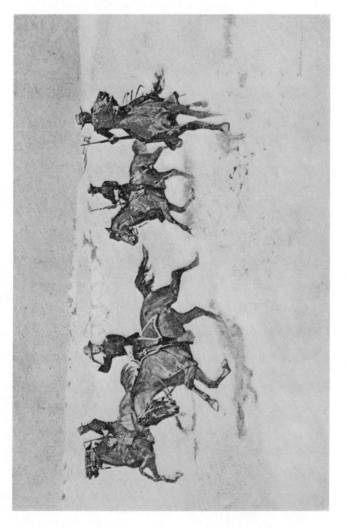

THE ADVANCE

"Say, Captain, I suppose Colonel Hamilton issues this order to get up at this hour, doesn't he?"

"He does."

"Well, he has to obey his own order, then, doesn't he?"

"He does."

I took a good long stretch and yawn, and what I said about Colonel Hamilton I will not commit to print, out of respect to the Colonel. Then I got up.

This bitterness of bed-parting passes. The Captain said he would put a "cook's police" under arrest for appearing in my make-up; but all these details will be forgotten, and whatever happens at this hour should be forgiven. I had just come from the North, where I had been sauntering over the territory of Montana with some Indians and a wild man from Virginia, getting up before light— tightening up on coffee and bacon for twelve hours in the saddle to prepare for more bacon and coffee; but at Adobe I had hoped for, even if I did not expect, some repose.

In the east there was a fine green coming over the sky. No one out of the painter guild would have admitted it was green, even on the rack, but what I mean is that you could not approach it in any other way. A nice little adjutant went jangling by on a hard-trotting thoroughbred, his shoulders high and his seat low. My old disease began to take possession of me; I could fairly feel the microbes generate. Another officer comes clattering, with his orderly following after. The fever has me. We mount, and we are off, all going to stables.

Out from the corrals swarm the troopers, leading their unwilling mounts. The horses are saying, " Damn the Colonel !" One of them comes in arching bounds; he is saying worse of the Colonel, or maybe only cussing out his own recruit for pulling his *cincha* too tight. They form troop lines in column, while the Captains throw open eyes over the things which would not interest my friend from New York or the German nurse-girl.

The two forward troops are the enemy, and are distinguished by wearing brown canvas stable-frocks. These shortly move out through the post, and are seen no more.

Now comes the sun. By the shades of Knickerbocker's *History of New York* I seem now to have gotten at the beginning; but patience, the sun is no detail out in the arid country. It does more things than blister your nose. It is the despair of the painter as it colors the minarets of the Bad Lands which abound around Adobe, and it dries up the company gardens if they don't

68

HORSE GYMNASTICS

watch the *acequias* mighty sharp. To one just out of bed it excuses existence. I find I begin to soften towards the Colonel. In fact, it is possible that he is entirely right about having his old trumpets blown around garrison at this hour, though it took the Captain's boot to prove it shortly since.

The command moves out, trotting quickly through the blinding clouds of dust. The landscape seems to get right up and mingle with the excitement. The supple, well-trained horses lose the scintillation on their coats, while Uncle Sam's blue is growing mauve very rapidly. But there is a useful look about the men, and the horses show condition after their long practice march just finished. Horses much used to go under saddle have well-developed quarters and strong stifle action. Fact is, nothing looks like a horse with a harness on. That is a job for mules, and these should have a labor organization and monopolize it.

The problem of the morning was that we as an advance were to drive the two troops which had gone on ahead. These in turn were to represent a rapidly retiring rear-guard. This training is more that troops may be handled with expedition, and that the men may gather the thing, rather than that officers should do brilliant things, which they might undertake on their own responsibility in time of war, such as pushing rapidly by on one flank and cutting out a rear-guard.

Grevious and very much to be commiserated is the task of the feeling historian who writes of these paper wars. He may see possibilities or calamities which do not signify. The morning orders provide against genius, and who will be able to estimate the surgical possibilities of blank cartridges? The sergeant-major cautioned me not to indicate by my actions what I saw as we rode to the top of a commanding hill. The enemy had abandoned the stream because their retreat would have been exposed to fire. They made a stand back in the hills. The advance felt the stream quickly, and passed, fanning out to develop. The left flank caught their fire, whereat the centre and right came around at top speed. But this is getting so serious.

The scene was crowded with little pictures, all happening quickly—little dots of horsemen gliding quickly along the yellow landscape, leaving long trails of steely dust in their wake. A scout comes trotting along, his face set in an expectant way, carbine advanced. A man on a horse is a vigorous, forceful thing to look at. It embodies the liveliness of nature in its most attractive form, especially when a gun and sabre are attached.

JUMPING ON A HORSE

When both living equations are young, full of oats and bacon, imbued with military ideas, and trained to the hour, it always seems to me that the ghost of a tragedy stalks at their side. This is why the polo-player does not qualify sentimentally. But what is one man beside two troops which come shortly in two solid chunks, with horses snorting and sending the dry landscape in a dusty pall for a quarter of a mile in the rear? It is good—ah! it is worth any one's while; but stop and think, what if we could magnify that? Tut, tut! as I said before, that only happens once in a generation. Adobe doesn't dream; it simply does its morning's work.

The rear-guard have popped at our advance, which exchanges with them. Their fire grows slack, and from our vantage we can see them mount quickly and flee.

After two hours of this we shake hands with the hostiles and trot home to breakfast.

These active, hard-riding, straight-shooting, open-order men are doing real work, and are not being stupefied by drill-ground routine, or rendered listless by file-closer prompting or sleepy reiteration.

By the time the command dismounts in front of stables we turn longingly to the thoughts of breakfast. Every one has completely forgiven the

Colonel, though I have no doubt he will be equally unpopular to-morrow morning.

But what do I see — am I faint? No; it has happened again. It looks as though I saw a soldier jump over a horse. I moved on him.

"Did I see you—" I began.

"Oh yes, sir—you see," returned a little soldier, who ran with the mincing steps of an athlete towards his horse, and landed standing up on his hind quarters, whereupon he settled down quietly into his saddle.

Others began to gyrate over and under their horses in a dizzy way. Some had taken their saddles off and now sat on their horses' bellies, while the big dog-like animals lay on their backs, with their feet in the air. It was circus business, or what they call "short and long horse" work—some not understandable phrase. Every one does it. While I am not unaccustomed to looking at cavalry, I am being perpetually surprised by the lengths to which our cavalry is carrying this Cossack drill. It is beginning to be nothing short of marvellous.

In the old days this thing was not known. Between building mud or log forts, working on the bull-train, marching or fighting, a man and a gun made a soldier; but it takes an education along with this now before he can qualify.

A TAME HORSE

The regular work at Adobe went on during the day—guard mount, orders, inspection, and routine.

At the club I was asked, " Going out this afternoon with us?"

" Yes, he is going; his horse will be up at 4.30; he wants to see this cavalry," answered my friend the Captain for me.

" Yes; it's fine moonlight. The Colonel is going to do an attack on Cossack posts out in the hills," said the adjutant.

So at five o'clock we again sallied out in the dust, the men in the ranks next me silhouetting one after the other more dimly until they disappeared in the enveloping cloud. They were cheerful, laughing and wondering one to another if Captain Garrard, the enemy, would get in on their pickets. He was regarded in the ranks as a sharp fellow, one to be well looked after.

At the line of hills where the Colonel stopped, the various troops were told off in their positions, while the long cool shadows of evening stole over the land, and the pale moon began to grow bolder over on the left flank.

I sat on a hill with a sergeant who knew history and horses. He remembered " Pansy," which had served sixteen years in the troop—and a first-rate old horse then; but a damned inspector with no soul came browsing around one day and condemned that old horse. Government got a measly ten dollars—or something like that. This ran along for a time ; when one day they were trooping up some lonely valley, and, behold, there stood " Pansy," as thin as a snake, tied by a wickieup. He greeted the troop with joyful neighs. The soldiers asked the Captain to be allowed to shoot him, but of course he said no. I could not learn if he winked when he said it. The column wound over the hill, a carbine rang from its rear, and " Pansy " lay down in the dust without a kick. Death is better than an Indian for a horse. The thing was not noticed at the time, but made a world of fuss afterwards, though how it all came out the sergeant did not develop, nor was it necessary.

Night settled down on the quiet hills, and the dark spots of pickets showed dimly on the gray surface of the land. The Colonel inspected his line, and found everybody alert and possessed of a good working knowledge of picket duties at night —one of the most difficult duties enlisted men have to perform. It is astonishing how short is the distance at which we can see a picket even in this bright night on the open hills.

I sat on my horse by a sergeant at a point in the line where I suspected the attack would come. The sergeant thought he saw figures moving in a

THE PURSUIT

dry bottom before us. I could not see. A column of dust off to the left indicated troops, but we thought it a ruse of Garrard's. My sergeant, though, had really seen the enemy, and said, softly, " They are coming."

The bottom twinkled and popped with savage little yellow winks; bang! went a rifle in my ear; " whew!" snorted my big horse; and our picket went to the supports clattering.

The shots and yells followed fast. The Colonel had withdrawn the supports towards the post rapidly, leaving his picket-line in the air—a thing which happens in war; but he did not lose much of that line, I should say.

It was an interesting drill. Pestiferous little man disturbed nature, and it all seemed so absurd out there on those quiet gray hills. It made me feel, as I slowed down and gazed at the vastness of things, like a superior sort of bug. In the middle distance several hundred troops are of no more proportion than an old cow bawling through the hills after her wolf-eaten calf. If my mental vision were not distorted I should never have seen the manœuvre at all — only the moon and the land doing what they have done before for so long a time.

We reached Adobe rather late, when I found that the day's work had done wonders for my appetite. I reminded the Captain that I had broken his bread but once that day.

" It is enough for a Ninth Cavalry man," he observed. However, I out-flanked this brutal disregard for established customs, but it was " cold."

In the morning I resisted the Captain's boot, and protested that I must be let alone; which being so, I appeared groomed and breakfasted at a Christian hour, fully persuaded that as between an Indian and a Ninth Cavalry man I should elect to be an Indian.

Some one must have disciplined the Colonel. I don't know who it was. There is only one woman in a post who can, generally; but no dinners were spoiled at Adobe by night-cat affairs.

Instead, during the afternoon we were to see Captain Garrard, the hostile, try to save two troops which were pressed into the bend of a river by throwing over a bridge, while holding the enemy in check. This was as complicated as putting a baby to sleep while reading law; so clearly my point of view was with the hostiles. With them I entered the neck. The horses were grouped in the brush, leaving some men who were going underground like gophers out near the entrance. The brown-canvas-covered soldiers grabbed their axes, rolled their eyes towards the open plain, and listened expectantly.

THE ATTACK ON THE COSSACK POSTS

The clear notes of a bugle rang; whackety, bang—clack—clack, went the axes. Trees fell all around. The forest seemed to drop on me. I got my horse and fled across the creek.

" That isn't fair; this stream is supposed to be impassable," sang out a lieutenant, who was doing a Blondin act on the first tree over, while beneath him yawned the chasm of four or five feet.

In less than a minute the whole forest got up again and moved towards the bridge. There were men behind it, but the leaves concealed them. Logs dropped over, brush piled on top. The rifles rang in scattered volleys, and the enemy's fire rolled out beyond the brush. No bullets whistled—that was a redeeming feature.

Aside from that it seemed as though every man was doing his ultimate act. They flew about; the shovels dug with despair; the sand covered the logs in a shower. While I am telling this the bridge was made.

The first horse came forward, led by his rider. He raised his eyes like St. Anthony; he did not approve of the bridge. He put his ears forward, felt with his toes, squatted behind, and made nervous side steps. The men moved on him in a solid crowd from behind. Stepping high and short he then bounded over, and after him in a stream came the willing brothers. Out along the bluffs strung

77

the troopers to cover the heroes who had held the neck, while they destroyed the bridge.

Then they rode home with the enemy, chaffing each other.

It is only a workaday matter, all this; but workaday stuff does the business nowadays.

MASSAI'S CROOKED TRAIL

IT is a bold person who will dare to say that a wilder savage ever lived than an Apache Indian, and in this respect no Apache can rival Massai.

He was a *bronco* Chiricahua whose *tequa* tracks were so long and devious that all of them can never be accounted for. Three regiments of cavalry, all the scouts—both white and black—and Mexicans galore had their hack, but the ghostly presence appeared and disappeared from the Colorado to the Yaqui. No one can tell how Massai's face looks, or looked, though hundreds know the shape of his footprint.

The Seventh made some little killings, but they fear that Massai was not among the game. There surely is or was such a person as Massai. He developed himself slowly, as I will show by the Sherlock Holmes methods of the chief of scouts, though even he only got so far, after all. Massai manifested himself like the dust-storm or the morning mist—a shiver in the air, and gone.

The chief walked his horse slowly back on the lost trail in disgust, while the scouts bobbed along behind perplexed. It was always so. Time has passed, and Massai, indeed, seems gone, since he appears no more. The hope in the breasts of countless men is nearly blighted; they no longer expect to see Massai's head brought into camp done up in an old shirt and dropped triumphantly on the ground in front of the chief of scouts' tent, so it is time to preserve what trail we can.

Three troops of the Tenth had gone into camp for the night, and the ghostly Montana landscape hummed with the murmur of many men. Supper was over, and I got the old Apache chief of scouts behind his own ducking, and demanded what he knew of an Apache Indian down in Arizona named Massai. He knew all or nearly all that any white man will ever know.

"All right," said the chief, as he lit a cigar and tipped his sombrero over his left eye, "but let me get it straight. Massai's trail was so crooked, I had to study nights to keep it arranged in my head. He didn't leave much more trail than a buzzard, anyhow, and it took years to unravel it. But I am anticipating.

"I was chief of scouts at Apache in the fall of '90, when word was brought in that an Indian

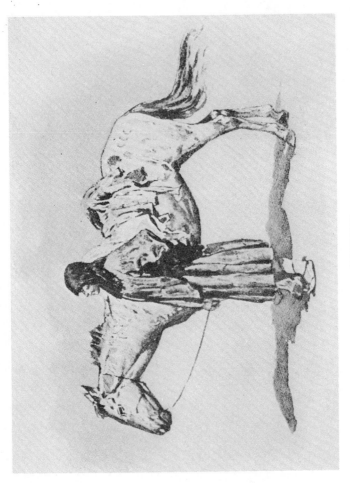

NATASTALE

girl named Natastale had disappeared, and that
her mother was found under a walnut-tree with
a bullet through her body. I immediately sent
Indian scouts to take the trail. They found the
tracks of a mare and colt going by the spot, and
thinking it would bring them to the girl, they followed it. Shortly they found a moccasin track
where a man had dismounted from the mare, and
without paying more attention to the horse track,
they followed it. They ran down one of my own
scouts in a *tiswin** camp, where he was carousing
with other drinkers. They sprang on him, got
him by the hair, disarmed and bound him. Then
they asked him what he had done with the girl,
and why he had killed the mother, to which he
replied that 'he did not know.' When he was
brought to me, about dark, there was intense excitement among the Indians, who crowded around
demanding Indian justice on the head of the murderer and ravisher of the women. In order to
save his life I took him from the Indians and
lodged him in the post guard-house. On the following morning, in order to satisfy myself positively that this man had committed the murder,
I sent my first sergeant, the famous Mickey Free,
with a picked party of trailers, back to the walnut-

---

* An intoxicating beverage made of corn.

tree, with orders to go carefully over the trail and run down the mare and colt, or find the girl, dead or alive, wherever they might.

" In two hours word was sent to me that the trail was running to the north. They had found the body of the colt with its throat cut, and were following the mare. The trail showed that a man afoot was driving the mare, and the scouts thought the girl was on the mare. This proved that we had the wrong man in custody. I therefore turned him loose, telling him he was all right. In return he told me that he owned the mare and colt, and that when he passed the tree the girl was up in its branches, shaking down nuts which her old mother was gathering. He had ridden along, and about an hour afterwards had heard a shot. He turned his mare loose, and proceeded on foot to the *tiswin* camp, where he heard later that the old woman had been shot and the girl 'lifted.' When arrested, he knew that the other scouts had trailed him from the walnut-tree ; he saw the circumstances against him, and was afraid.

" On the night of the second day Mickey Free's party returned, having run the trail to within a few hundred yards of the camp of Alcashay in the Forestdale country, between whose band and the band to which the girl belonged there was a blood-feud. They concluded that the murderer belonged

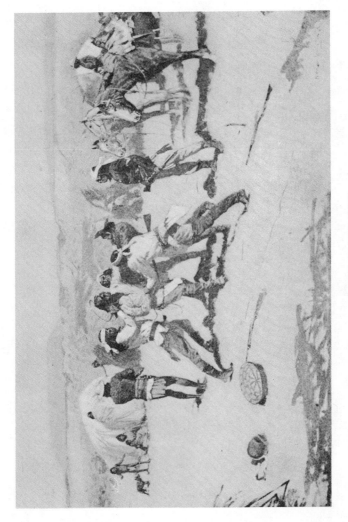

THE ARREST OF THE SCOUT

to Alcashay's camp, and were afraid to engage him.

" I sent for Alcashay to come in immediately, which he did, and I demanded that he trail the man and deliver him up to me, or I would take my scout corps, go to his camp, and arrest all suspicious characters. He stoutly denied that the man was in his camp, promised to do as I directed, and, to further allay any suspicions, he asked for my picked trailers to help run the trail. With this body of men he proceeded on the track, and they found that it ran right around his camp, then turned sharply to the east, ran within two hundred yards of a stage - ranch, thence into some rough mountain country, where it twisted and turned for forty miles. At this point they found the first camp the man had made. He had tied the girl to a tree by the feet, which permitted her to sleep on her back; the mare had been killed, some steaks taken out, and some meat ' jerked.' From thence on they could find no trail which they could follow. At long intervals they found his moccasin mark between rocks, but after circling for miles they gave it up. In this camp they found and brought to me a fire-stick—the first and only one I had ever seen—and they told me that the fire-stick had not been used by Apaches for many years. There were only a few old men in my camp who were familiar with its use, though one managed to light his cigarette with it. They reasoned from this that the man was a bronco Indian who had been so long ' out ' that he could not procure matches, and also that he was a much wilder one than any of the Indians then known to be outlawed.

" In about a week there was another Indian girl stolen from one of my hay-camps, and many scouts thought it was the same Indian, who they decided was one of the well-known outlaws ; but older and better men did not agree with them ; so there the matter rested for some months.

" In the spring the first missing girl rode into Fort Apache on a fine horse, which was loaded down with buckskins and other Indian finery. Two cowboys followed her shortly and claimed the pony, which bore a C C C brand, and I gave it up to them. I took the girl into my office, for she was so tired that she could hardly stand up, while she was haggard and worn to the last degree. When she had sufficiently recovered she told me her story. She said she was up in the walnut-tree when an Indian shot her mother, and coming up, forced her to go with him. He trailed and picked up the mare, bound her on its back, and drove it along. The colt whinnied, whereupon he cut its throat. He made straight for Alcashay's camp,

which he circled, and then turned sharply to the
east, where he made the big twisting through the
mountains which my scouts found. After going
all night and the next day, he made the first camp.
After killing and cooking the mare, he gave her
something to eat, tied her up by the feet, and
standing over her, told her that he was getting to
be an old man, was tired of making his own fires,
and wanted a woman. If she was a good girl he
would not kill her, but would treat her well and
always have venison hanging up. He continued
that he was going away for a few hours, and would
come back and kill her if she tried to undo the
cords; but she fell asleep while he was talking.
After daylight he returned, untied her, made her
climb on his back, and thus carried her for a long
distance. Occasionally he made her alight where
the ground was hard, telling her if she made any
'sign' he would kill her, which made her careful
of her steps.

" After some miles of this blinding of the trail
they came upon a white horse that was tied to a
tree. They mounted double, and rode all day as
fast as he could lash the pony, until, near nightfall, it fell from exhaustion, whereupon he killed it
and cooked some of the carcass. The bronco Indian took himself off for a couple of hours, and
when he returned, brought another horse, which

they mounted, and sped onward through the moonlight all night long. On that morning they were in the high mountains, the poor pony suffering the same fate as the others.

" They stayed here two days, he tying her up whenever he went hunting, she being so exhausted after the long flight that she lay comatose in her bonds. From thence they journeyed south slowly, keeping to the high mountains, and only once did he speak, when he told her that a certain mountain pass was the home of the Chiricahuas. From the girl's account she must have gone far south into the Sierra Madre of Old Mexico, though of course she was long since lost.

" He killed game easily, she tanned the hides, and they lived as man and wife. Day by day they threaded their way through the deep cañons and over the Blue Mountain ranges. By this time he had become fond of the White Mountain girl, and told her that he was Massai, a Chiricahua warrior; that he had been arrested after the Geronimo war and sent East on the railroad over two years since, but had escaped one night from the train, and had made his way alone back to his native deserts. Since then it is known that an Indian did turn up missing, but it was a big band of prisoners, and some births had occurred, which made the checking off come

SCOUTS

straight. He was not missed at the time. From
what the girl said, he must have got off east of
Kansas City and travelled south and then west,
till at last he came to the lands of the Mescalero
Apaches, where he stayed for some time. He was
over a year making this journey, and told the girl
that no human eye ever saw him once in that
time. This is all he ever told the girl Natastale,
and she was afraid to ask him more. Beyond
these mere facts, it is still a midnight prowl of
a human coyote through a settled country for
twelve hundred miles, the hardihood of the un-
dertaking being equalled only by the instinct
which took him home.

"Once only while the girl was with him did
they see sign of other Indians, and straightway
Massai turned away — his wild nature shunning
even the society of his kind.

"At times 'his heart was bad,' and once he sat
brooding for a whole day, finally telling her that
he was going into a bad country to kill Mexicans,
that women were a burden on a warrior, and that
he had made up his mind to kill her. All through
her narrative he seemed at times to be overcome
with this blood-thirst, which took the form of a
homicidal melancholia. She begged so hard for
her life that he relented ; so he left her in the wild
tangle of mountains while he raided on the Mexi-

can settlements. He came back with horses and powder and lead. This last was in Winchester bullets, which he melted up and recast into .50-calibre balls made in moulds of cactus sticks. He did not tell how many murders he had committed during these raids, but doubtless many.

" They lived that winter through in the Sierras, and in the spring started north, crossing the railroad twice, which meant the Guaymas and the Southern Pacific. They sat all one day on a high mountain and watched the trains of cars go by; but ' his heart got bad ' at the sight of them, and again he concluded to kill the girl. Again she begged off, and they continued up the range of the Mogollons. He was unhappy in his mind during all this journey, saying men were scarce up here, that he must go back to Mexico and kill some one.

" He was tired of the woman, and did not want her to go back with him, so, after sitting all day on a rock while she besought him, the old wolf told her to go home in peace. But the girl was lost, and told him that either the Mexicans or Americans would kill her if she departed from him; so his mood softened, and telling her to come on, he began the homeward journey. They passed through a small American town in the middle of the night—he having previously taken

88

THE CHIEF OF SCOUTS

off the Indian rawhide shoes from the ponies. They crossed the Gila near the Nau Taw Mountains. Here he stole two fresh horses, and loading one with all the buckskins, he put her on and headed her down the Eagle Trail to Black River. She now knew where she was, but was nearly dying from the exhaustion of his fly-by-night expeditions. He halted her, told her to 'tell the white officer that she was a pretty good girl, better than the San Carlos woman, and that he would come again and get another.' He struck her horse and was gone.

" Massai then became a problem to successive chiefs of scouts, a bugbear to the reservation Indians, and a terror to Arizona. If a man was killed or a woman missed, the Indians came galloping and the scouts lay on his trail. If he met a woman in the defiles, he stretched her dead if she did not please his errant fancy. He took pot-shots at the men ploughing in their little fields, and knocked the Mexican bull-drivers on the head as they plodded through the blinding dust of the Globe Road. He even sat like a vulture on the rim-rock and signalled the Indians to come out and talk. When two Indians thus accosted did go out, they found themselves looking down Massai's .50-calibre, and were tempted to do his bidding. He sent one in for sugar and coffee, holding the brother, for such he happened to be, as a hostage till the sugar and coffee came. Then he told them that he was going behind a rock to lie down, cautioning them not to move for an hour. That was an unnecessary bluff, for they did not wink an eye till sundown. Later than this he stole a girl in broad daylight in the face of a San Carlos camp and dragged her up the rocks. Here he was attacked by fifteen or twenty bucks, whom he stood off until darkness. When they reached his lair in the morning, there lay the dead girl, but Massai was gone.

" I never saw Massai but once, and then it was only a piece of his G string flickering in the brush. We had followed his trail half the night, and just at daylight, as we ascended a steep part of the mountains, I caught sight of a pony's head looking over a bush. We advanced rapidly, only to find the horse grunting from a stab wound in the belly, and the little camp scattered around about him. The shirt tail flickering in the brush was all of Massai. We followed on, but he had gone down a steep bluff. We went down too, thus exposing ourselves to draw his fire so that we could locate him, but he was not tempted.

" The late Lieutenant Clark had much the same view of this mountain outlaw, and since those days two young men of the Seventh Cavalry, Rice and

Averill, have on separate occasions crawled on his
camp at the break of day, only to see Massai go
out of sight in the brush like a blue quail.

"Lieutenant Averill, after a forced march of
eighty-six miles, reached a hostile camp near
morning, after climbing his detachment, since
midnight, up the almost inaccessible rocks, in
hopes of surprising the camp. He divided his
force into three parts, and tried, as well as possible, to close every avenue of escape; but as the
camp was on a high rocky hill at the junction of
four deep cañons, this was found impracticable.
At daylight the savages came out together, running like deer, and making for the cañons. The
soldiers fired, killing a buck and accidentally
wounding a squaw, but Massai simply disappeared.

"That's the story of Massai. It is not as long
as his trail," said the chief of scouts.

JOSHUA GOODENOUGH'S OLD

LETTER

THE following letter has come into my possession, which I publish because it is history, and
descends to the list of those humble beings who
builded so well for us the institutions which we
now enjoy in this country.   It is yellow with age,
and much frayed out at the foldings, being in those
spots no longer discernible.   It runs:

ALBANY *June* 1798.

To MY DEAR SON JOSEPH.—It is true that there
are points in the history of the country in which
your father had a concern in his early life, and as
you ask me to put it down I will do so briefly.
Not, however, my dear Joseph, as I was used to
tell it to you when you were a lad, but with more
exact truth, for I am getting on in my years and
this will soon be all that my posterity will have of
their ancestor.   I conceive that now the descend-

ents of the noble band of heroes who fought off the indians, the Frenche and the British will prevail in this country, and my children's children may want to add what is found here in written to their own achievements.

To begin with, my father was the master of a fishing-schooner, of Marblehead. In the year 1745 he was taken at sea by a French man-of-war off Louisbourg, after making a desperate resistence. His ship was in a sinking condition and the blood was mid-leg deep on her deck. Your grandfather was an upstanding man and did not prostrate easily, but the Frencher was too big, so he was captured and later found his way as a prisoner to Quebec. He was exchanged by a mistake in his identity for Huron indians captivated in York, and he subsequently settled near Albany, afterwards bringing my mother, two sisters, and myself from Marblehead.

He engaged in the indian trade, and as I was a rugged lad of my years I did often accompany him on his expeditions westward into the Mohawk townes, thus living in bark camps among Indians and got thereby a knowledge of their ways. I made shift also to learn their language, and what with living in the bush for so many years I was a hand at a pack or paddle and no mean hunter besides. I was put to school for two seasons in

93

CROOKED TRAILS

Albany which was not to my liking, so I straightway ran off to a hunters camp up the Hudson,
and only came back when my father would say
that I should not be again put with the pedegogue.
For this adventure I had a good strapping from
my father, and was set to work in his trade again.
My mother was a pious woman and did not like
me to grow up in the wilderness—for it was the
silly fashion of those times to ape the manners and
dress of the Indians.

My father was a shifty trader and very ventur-
some. He often had trouble with the people in
these parts, who were Dutch and were jealous of
him. He had a violent temper and was not easily
bent from his purpose by opporsition. His men
had a deal of fear of him and good cause enough
in the bargain, for I once saw him discipline a
half-negro man who was one of his boat-men for
stealing his private jug of liquor from his private
pack. He clinched with the negro and soon had
him on the ground, where the man struggled man-
fully but to no purpose, for your grandfather soon
had him at his mercy. " Now," said he, " give me
the jug or take the consequences." The other
boat paddlers wanted to rescue him, but I menaced
them with my fusil and the matter ended by the
return of the jug.

In 1753 he met his end at the hands of western

indians in the French interest, who shot him as he was helping to carry a battoe, and he was burried in the wilderness. My mother then returned to her home in Massassachusetts, journeying with a party of traders but I staid with the Dutch on these frontiers because I had learned the indian trade and liked the country. Not having any chances, I had little book learning in my youth, having to this day a regret concerning it. I read a few books, but fear I had a narrow knowledge of things outside the Dutch settlements. On the frontiers, for that matter, few people had much skill with the pen, nor was much needed. The axe and rifle, the paddle and pack being more to our hands in those rough days. To prosper though, men weare shrewd-headed enough. I have never seen that books helped people to trade sharper. Shortly afterwards our trade fell away, for the French had embroiled the Indians against us. Crown Point was the Place from which the Indians in their interest had been fitted out to go against our settlements, so a design was formed by His Majesty the British King to dispossess them of that place. Troops were levid in the Province and the war began. The Frenchers had the best of the fighting.

Our frontiers were beset with the Canada indians so that it was not safe to go about in the country at all. I was working for Peter Vrooman, a trader, and was living at his house on the Mohawk. One Sunday morning I found a negro boy who was shot through the body with two balls as he was hunting for stray sheep, and all this within half a mile of Vrooman's house. Then an express came up the valley who left word that the Province was levying troops at Albany to fight the French, and I took my pay from Vrooman saying that I would go to Albany for a soldier. Another young man and myself paddled down to Albany, and we both enlisted in the York levies. We drawed our ammunition, tents, kettles, bowls and knives at the Albany flats, and were drilled by an officer who had been in her Majesty's Service. One man was given five hundred lashes for enlisting in some Connecticut troops, and the orders said that any man who should leave His Majesty's service without a Regular discharge should suffer Death. The restraint which was put upon me by this military life was not to my liking, and I was in a mortal dread of the whippings which men were constantly receiving for breaches of the discipline. I felt that I could not survive the shame of being trussed up and lashed before men's eyes, but I did also have a great mind to fight the French which kept me along. One day came an order to prepare a list of officers and men who were willing to go

"I DID NOT CONCEIVE THAT THEY WERE MUCH FITTED FOR BUSH-RANGING"

scouting and be freed from other duty, and after some time I got my name put down, for I was thought too young, but I said I knew the woods, had often been to Andiatirocte (or Lake George as it had then become the fashion to call it) and they let me go. It was dangerous work, for reports came every day of how our Rangers suffered up country at the hands of the cruel savages from Canada, but it is impossible to play at bowls without meeting some rubs. A party of us proceeded up river to join Captain Rogers at Fort Edward, and we were put to camp on an Island. This was in October of the year 1757. We found the Rangers were rough borderers like ourselvs, mostly Hampshire men well used to the woods and much accustomed to the Enemy. They dressed in the fashion of those times in skin and grey duffle hunting frocks, and were well armed. Rogers himself was a doughty man and had a reputation as a bold Ranger leader. The men declaired that following him was sore service, but that he most always met with great success. The Fort was garrissoned by His Majesty's soldiers, and I did not conceive that they were much fitted for bush-ranging, which I afterwards found to be the case, but they would always fight well enough, though often to no good purpose, which was not their fault so much as the headstrong leadership which persisted in making them come to close quarters while at a disadvantage. There were great numbers of pack horses coming and going with stores, and many officers in gold lace and red coats were riding about directing here and there. I can remember that I had a great interest in this concourse of men, for up to that time I had not seen much of the world outside of the wilderness. There was terror of the Canada indians who had come down to our borders hunting for scalps—for these were continually lurking near the cantanements to waylay the unwary. I had got acquainted with a Hampshire borderer who had passed his life on the Canada frontier, where he had fought indians and been captured by them. I had seen much of indians and knew their silent forest habits when hunting, so that I felt that when they were after human beings they would be no mean adversaries, but I had never hunted them or they me.

I talked at great length with this Shankland, or Shanks as he was called on account of his name and his long legs, in course of which he explained many useful points to me concerning Ranger ways. He said they always marched until it was quite dark before encamping—that they always returned by a different route from that on which they went out, and that they circled on their trail at intervals so that they might intercept any one coming on their rear. He told me not to gather up close to other Rangers in a fight but to keep spread out, which gave the Enemy less mark to fire upon and also deceived them as to your own numbers. Then also he cautioned me not to fire on the Enemy when we were in ambush till they have approached quite near, which will put them in greater surprise and give your own people time to rush in on them with hatchets or cutlasses. Shanks and I had finally a great fancy for each other and passed most of our time in company. He was a slow man in his movements albeit he could move fast enough on occassion, and was a great hand to take note of things happening around him. No indian was better able to discern a trail in the bush than he, nor could one be found his equal at making snow shoes, carving a powder horn or fashioning any knick-nack he was a mind to set his hand to.

The Rangers were accustomed to scout in small parties to keep the Canada indians from coming close to Fort Edward. I had been out with Shanks on minor occasions, but I must relate my first adventure.

A party ... (here the writing is lost) ... was desirous of taking a captive or scalp. I misdoubted our going alone by ourselvs, but he said we were as safe as with more. We went northwest slowly for two days, and though we saw many old trails we found none which were fresh. We had gone on until night when we lay bye near a small brook. I was awakened by Shanks in the night and heard a great howling of wolves at some distance off togther with a gun shot. We lay awake until daybreak and at intervals heard a gun fired all though the night. We decided that the firing could not come from a large party and so began to approach the sound slowly and with the greatest caution. We could not understand why the wolves should be so bold with the gun firing, but as we came neare we smelled smoke and knew it was a camp-fire. There were a number of wolves running about in the underbrush from whose actions we located the camp. From a rise we could presently see it, and were surprised to find it contained five Indians all lying asleep in their blankets. The wolves would go right up to the camp and yet the indians did not deign to give them any notice whatsoever, or even to move in the least when one wolf pulled at the blanket of a sleeper. We each selected a man when we had come near enough, and preparing to deliver our fire, when of a sudden one figure rose up slightly. We nevertheless fired and then rushed forward, reloading. To our astonishment none of the figures moved in the least but the

THE MARCH OF ROGERS'S RANGERS

wolves scurried off. We were advancing cautiously when Shanks caught me by the arm saying " we must run, that they had all died of the small-pox," and run we did lustily for a good long distance. After this manner did many Indians die in the wilderness from that dreadful disease, and I have since supposed that the last living indian had kept firing his gun at the wolves until he had no longer strength to reload his piece.

After this Shanks and I had become great friends for he had liked the way I had conducted myself on this expedition. He was always arguying with me to cut off my eel-skin que which I wore after the fashion of the Dutch folks, saying that the Canada indians would parade me for a Dutchman after that token was gone with my scalp. He had . . . . (writing obliterated).

Early that winter I was one of 150 Rangers who marched with Captain Rogers against the Enemy at Carrillion. The snow was not deep at starting but it continued to snow until it was heavy footing and many of the men gave out and returned to Fort Edward, but notwithstanding my exhaustion I continued on for six days until we were come to within six hundred yards of Carrillion Fort. The captain had made us a speech in which he told us the points where we were to rendevoux if we were broke in the fight, for further resistence until night came on, when we could take ourselvs off as best we might. I was with the advance guard. We lay in ambush in some fallen timber quite close to a road, from which we could see the smoke from the chimneys of the Fort and the centries walking their beats. A French soldier was seen to come from the Fort and the word was passed to let him go bye us, as he came down the road. We lay perfectly still not daring to breathe, and though he saw nothing he stopped once and seemed undecided as to going on, but suspecting nothing he continued and was captured by our people below, for prisoners were wanted at Headquarters to give information of the French forces and intentions. A man taken in this way was threatened with Death if he did not tell the whole truth, which under the circumstancs he mostly did to save his life.

The French did not come out of the Fort after us, though Rogers tried to entice them by firing guns and showing small parties of men which feigned to retreat. We were ordered to destroy what we could of the supplies, so Shanks and I killed a small cow which we found in the edge of the clearing and took off some fresh beef of which food we were sadly in need, for on these scouts the Rangers were not permitted to fire guns at game though it was found in thir path, as it often was in fact. I can remember on one occassion that I stood by a tree in a snow storm, with my gun depressed under my frock the better to keep it dry, when I was minded to glance quickly around and there saw a large wolf just ready to spring upon me. I cautiously presented my fusee but did not dare to fire against the orders. An other Ranger came shortly into view and the wolf took himself off. We burned some large wood piles, which no doubt made winter work for to keep some Frenchers at home. They only fired some cannon at us, which beyond a great deal of noise did no harm. We then marched back to Fort Edward and were glad enough to get there, since it was time for snow-shoes, which we had not with us.

The Canada indians were coming down to our Forts and even behind them to intercept our convoys or any parties out on the road, so that the Rangers were kept out, to head them when they could, or get knowledge of their whereabouts. Shanks and I went out with two Mohegon indians on a scout. It was exceedingly stormy weather and very heavy travelling except on the River. I had got a bearskin blanket from the indians which is necessary to keep out the cold at this season. We had ten days of bread, pork and rum with a little salt with us, and followed the indians in a direction North-and-bye-East towards the lower end of Lake Champlain, always keeping to the high-ground with the falling snow to fill our tracks behind us. For four days we travelled when we were well up the west side. We had crossed numbers of trails but they were all full of old snow and not worth regarding—still we were so far from our post that in event of encountering any numbers of the Enemy we had but small hope of a safe return and had therefore to observe the greatest caution.

As we were making our way an immense painter so menaced us that we were forced to fire our guns to dispatch him. He was found to be very old, his teeth almost gone, and was in the last stages of starvation. We were much alarmed at this misadventure, fearing the Enemy might hear us or see the ravens gathering above, so we crossed the Lake that night on some new ice to blind our trail, where I broke through in one place and was only saved by Shanks, who got hold of my eel-skin que, thereby having something to pull me out with. We got into a deep gully, and striking flint made a fire to dry me and I did not suffer much inconvenience.

The day following we took a long circle and came out on the lower end of the Lake, there laying two days in ambush, watching the Lake for any parties coming or going. Before dark a Mohigon came in from watch saying that men were coming down the Lake. We gathered at the point and saw seven of the Enemy come slowly on. There were three indians two Canadians and a French officer. Seeing they would shortly pass under our point of land we made ready to fire, and did deliver one fire as they came nigh, but the guns of our Mohigons failed to explode, they being old and well nigh useless, so that all the damage we did was to kill one indian and wound a Canadian, who was taken in hand by his companions who made off down the shore and went into the bush. We tried to head them unsuccessfully, and after examining the guns of our indians we feared they were so disabled that we gave up and retreated down the Lake, travelling all night. Near morning we saw a small fire which we spied out only to find a large party of the Enemy, whereat we were much disturbed, for our travelling had exhausted us and we feared the pursuit of a fresh enemy as soon as morning should come to show them our trail. We then made our way as fast as possible until late that night, when we laid down for refreshment. We built no fire but could not sleep for fear of the Enemy for it was a bright moonlight, and sure enough we had been there but a couple of hours when we saw the Enemy coming on our track. We here abandoned our bear - skins with what provissions we had left and ran back on our trail toward the advancing party. It was dark in the forest and we hoped they might not discover our back track for some time, thus giving us a longer start. This ruse was successful. After some hours travel I became so exhausted that I stopped to rest, whereat the Mohigans left us, but Shanks bided with me, though urging me to move forward. After a time I got strength to move on. Shanks said the Canadians would come up with us if we did not make fast going of it, and that they would disembowel us or tie us to a tree and burn us as was their usual way, for we could in no wise hope to make head against so large a party. Thus we walked steadily till high noon, when my wretched strength gave out so that I fell down saying I had as leave die there as elsewhere. Shanks followed back on our trail, while I fell into a drouse but was so sore I could not sleep. After a time I heard a shot, and shortly two more, when Shanks came running back to me. He had killed an advancing indian and stopped them for a moment. He kicked me vigorously, telling me to come on, as the indians would soon come on again. I got up, and though I could scarcely move I was minded diligently to persevere after

Shanks. Thus we staggered on until near night time, when we again stopped and I fell into a deep sleep, but the enemy did not again come up. On the following day we got into Fort Edward, where I was taken with a distemper, was seized with very grevious pains in the head and back and a fever. They let blood and gave me a physic, but I did not get well around for some time. For this sickness I have always been thankful, otherwise I should have been with Major Rogers in his unfortunate battle, which has become notable enough, where he was defeated by the Canadians and Indians and lost nigh all his private men, only escaping himself by a miracle. We mourned the loss of many friends who were our comrades, though it was not the fault of any one, since the Enemy had three times the number of the Rangers and hemmed them in. Some of the Rangers had surrendered under promise of Quarter, but we afterwards heard that they were tied to trees and hacked to death because the indians had found a scalp in the breast of a man's hunting frock, thus showing that we could never expect such bloody minded villiains to keep their promises of Quarter.

I was on several scouts against them that winter but encountered nothing worthy to relate excepting the hardships which fell to a Ranger's lot. In

June the Army having been gathered we proceeded under Abercromby up the Lake to attack Ticonderoga. I thought at the time that so many men must be invincible, but since the last war I have been taught to know different. There were more Highlanders, Grenadiers, Provincial troops, Artillery and Rangers than the eye could compass, for the Lake was black with their battoes. This concourse proceeded to Ticondaroga where we had a great battle and lost many men, but to no avail since we were forced to return.

The British soldiers were by this time made servicible for forest warfare, since the officers and men had been forced to rid themselvs of their useless incumbrances and had cut off the tails of their long coats till they scarcely reached below thir middles—they had also left the women at the Fort, browned thir gun barrells and carried thir provisions on their backs, each man enough for himself, as was our Ranger custom. The army was landed at the foot of the Lake, where the Rangers quickly drove off such small bodies of Frenchers and Indians as opposed us, and we began our march by the rapids. Rogers men cleared the way and had a most desperate fight with some French who were minded to stop us, but we shortly killed and captured most of them. We again fell in with them that afternoon and

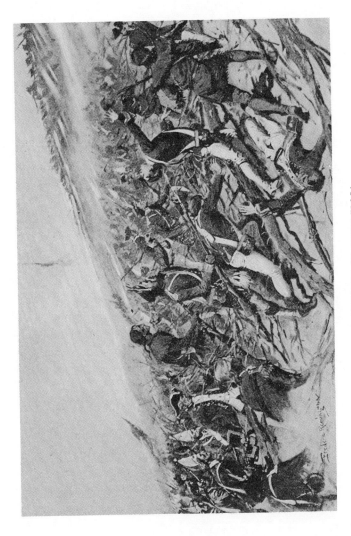

THE STORMING OF TICONDEROGA

were challenged Qui vive but answered that we were French, but they were not deceived and fired upon us, after which a hot skirmish insued during which Lord Howe was shot through the breast, for which we were all much depressed, because he was our real leader and had raised great hopes of success for us. The Rangers had liked him because he was wont to spend much time talking with them in thir camps and used also to go on scouts. The Rangers were not over fond of British officers in general.

When the time had come for battle we Rangers moved forward, accompanied by the armed boat-men and the Provincial troops. We drove in the French pickets and came into the open where the trees were felled tops toward us in a mighty abbatis, as thiough blown down by the wind. It was all we could undertake to make our way through the mass, and all the while the great breast-works of the French belched cannon and musket balls while the limbs and splinters flew around us. Then out of the woods behind us is-sued the heavy red masses of the British troops ad-vancing in battle array with purpose to storm with the bayonet. The maze of fallen trees with their withered leaves hanging broke their ranks, and the French Retrenchment blazed fire and death. They advanced bravely up but all to no good purpose, and hundreds there met their death. My dear Joseph I have the will but not the way to tell you all I saw that awful afternoon. I have since been in many battles and skirmishes, but I never have witnessed such slaughter and such wild fighting as the British storm of Ticondaroga. We became mixed up—Highlanders, Grenadiers, Light Troops, Rangers and all, and we beat against that mass of logs and maze of fallend timber and we beat in vain. I was once carried right up to the breastwork, but we were stopped by the bristling mass of sharpened branches, while the French fire swept us front and flank. The ground was covered deep with dying men, and as I think it over now I can remember nothing but the fruit bourne by the tree of war, for I looked upon so many wonderous things that July day that I could not set them downe at all. We drew off after seeing that human valor could not take that work. We Rangers then skirmished with the French colony troops and the Canada indians until dark while our people rescued the wounded, and then we fell back. The Army was utterly demoralized and made a headlong retreat, during which many wounded men were left to die in the woods. Shanks and I paddled a light bark canoe down the Lake next day, in the bottom of which lay a wounded British officer attended by his servant.

PADDLING THE WOUNDED BRITISH OFFICER

I took my discharge, and lived until the following Spring with Vrooman at German Flats, when I had a desire to go again to the more active service of the Rangers, for living in camps and scouting, notwithstanding its dangers, was agreeable to my taste in those days. So back to Albany I started, and there met Major Rogers, whom I acquainted with my desire to again join his service, whereat he seemed right glad to put me downe. I accordingly journeyed to Crown Point, where I went into camp. I had bought me a new fire-lock at Albany which was provided with a bayonet. It was short, as is best fitted for the bush, and about 45 balls to the pound. I had shot it ten times on trial and it had not failed to discharge at each pull. There was a great change in the private men of the Rangers, so many old ones had been frost bitten and gone home. I found my friend Shanks, who had staid though he had been badly frosted during the winter. He had such a hate of the Frenchers and particularly of the Canada Indians that he would never cease to fight them, they having killed all his relatives in New Hampshire which made him bitter against them, he always saying that they might as well kill him and thus make an end of the family.

In June I went north down Champlain with 250 Rangers and Light Infantry in sloop-vessels.

The Rangers were .... (writing lost) .... but it made no difference. The party was landed on the west side of the Lake near Isle au Noix and lay five days in the bush, it raining hard all the time. I was out with a recoinnoitering party to watch the Isle, and very early in the morning we saw the French coming to our side in boats, whereat we acquainted Major Rogers that the French were about to attack us. We were drawn up in line to await their coming. The forest always concealed a Ranger line, so that there might not have been a man within a hundred miles for all that could be seen, and so it was that an advance party of the Enemy walked into our line and were captured, which first appraised the French of our position. They shortly attacked us on our left, but I was sent with a party to make our way through a swamp in order to attack their rear. This we accomplished so quietly that we surprized some Canada indians who were lying back of the French line listening to a prophet who was incanting. These we slew, and after our firing many French grenadiers came running past, when they broke before our line. I took a Frenchman prisoner, but he kept his bayonet pointed at me, all the time yelling in French which I did not understand, though I had my loaded gun pointed at him. He seemed to be disturbed at the sight of a scalp

THE CAPTURE OF THE FRENCH GRENADIER

which I had hanging in my belt. I had lately took it from the head of an Indian, it being my first, but I was not minded to kill the poor Frenchman and was saying so in English. He put down his fire-lock finally and offered me his flask to drink liquor with him, but I did not use it. I had known that Shanks carried poisoned liquor in his pack, with the hope that it would destroy any indians who might come into possession of it, if he was taken, whether alive or dead. As I was escorting the Frenchman back to our boats he quickly ran away from me, though I snapped my fire-lock at him, which failed to explode, it having become wet from the rain. Afterwards I heard that a Ranger had shot him, seeing him running in the bush.

We went back to our boats after this victory and took all our wounded and dead with us, which last we buried on an island. Being joined by a party of Stockbridge Indians we were again landed, and after marching for some days came to a road where we recoinnoitered St. John's Fort but did not attack it, Rogers judging it not to be takeable with our force. From here we began to march so fast that only the strongest men could keep up, and at day-break came to another Fort. We ran into the gate while a hay-waggon was passing through, and surprised and captured all the garrison, men women and children. After we had burned and destroyed everything we turned the women and children adrift, but drove the men along as prisoners, making them carry our packs. We marched so fast that the French grenadiers could not keep up, for their breeches were too tight for them to march with ease, whereat we cut off the legs of them with our knives, when they did better.

After this expedition we scouted from Crown Point in canoes, Shanks and myself going as far north as we dared toward Isle au Noix, and one day while lying on the bank we saw the army coming. It was an awsome sight to see so many boats filled with brave uniforms, as they danced over the waves. The Rangers and indians came a half a mile ahead of the Army in whale-boats all in line abreast, while behind them came the light Infantry and Grenadiers with Provincial troops on the flanks and Artillery and Store boats bringing up the Rear.

Shanks and I fell in with the Ranger boats, being yet in our small bark and much hurled about by the waves, which rolled prodigious.

The Army continued up the Lake and drove the Frenchers out of their Forts, they not stopping to resist us till we got to Chamblee, where we staid. But the French in Canada had all

surrendered to the British and the war was over.
This ended my service as a Ranger in those parts.
I went back to Vroomans intending to go again
into the indian trade, for now we hoped that the
French would no longer be able to stop our en-
terprises.

Now my dear son—I will send you this long
letter, and will go on writing of my later life in
the Western country and in the War of Inde-
pendence, and will send you those letters as soon
as I have them written. I did not do much or
occupy a commanding position, but I served
faithfully in what I had to do. For the present
God bless you my dear son.

JOSHUA GOODENOUGH.

CRACKER COWBOYS OF
FLORIDA

ONE can thresh the straw of history until he is
well worn out, and also is running some risk of
wearing others out who may have to listen, so I
will waive the telling of who the first cowboy was,
even if I knew; but the last one who has come
under my observation lives down in Florida, and
the way it happened was this: I was sitting in a
" sto' do'," as the " Crackers " say, waiting for the
clerk to load some "number eights," when my
friend said, " Look at the cowboys!" This immediately caught my interest. With me cowboys are what gems and porcelains are to some
others. Two very emaciated Texas ponies pat-
tered down the street, bearing wild-looking in-
dividuals, whose hanging hair and drooping hats
and generally bedraggled appearance would re-
mind you at once of the Spanish-moss which
hangs so quietly and helplessly to the limbs of

"ABOUT FOUR DOLLARS WORTH OF CLOTHES BETWEEN THEM"

the oaks out in the swamps. There was none of the bilious fierceness and rearing plunge which I had associated with my friends out West, but as a fox-terrier is to a yellow cur, so were these last. They had on about four dollars' worth of clothes between them, and rode McClellan saddles, with saddle-bags, and guns tied on before. The only things they did which were conventional were to tie their ponies up by the head in brutal disregard, and then get drunk in about fifteen minutes. I could see that in this case, while some of the tail feathers were the same, they would easily classify as new birds.

"And so you have cowboys down here?" I said to the man who ran the meat-market.

He picked a tiny piece of raw liver out of the meshes of his long black beard, tilted his big black hat, shoved his arms into his white apron front, and said:

"Gawd! yes, stranger; I was one myself."

The plot thickened so fast that I was losing much, so I became more deliberate. "Do the boys come into town often?" I inquired further.

"Oh yes, 'mos' every little spell," replied the butcher, as he reached behind his weighing-scales and picked up a double-barrelled shot-gun, sawed off. "We-uns are expectin' of they-uns to-day."

And he broke the barrels and took out the shells to examine them.

"Do they come shooting?" I interposed.

He shut the gun with a snap. "We split even, stranger."

Seeing that the butcher was a fragile piece of bric-à-brac, and that I might need him for future study, I bethought me of the banker down the street. Bankers are bound to be broad-gauged, intelligent, and conservative, so I would go to him and get at the ancient history of this neck of woods. I introduced myself, and was invited behind the counter. The look of things reminded me of one of those great green terraces which conceal fortifications and ugly cannon. It was boards and wire screen in front, but behind it were shot-guns and six-shooters hung in the handiest way, on a sort of disappearing gun-carriage arrangement. Shortly one of the cowboys of the street scene floundered in. He was two-thirds drunk, with brutal, shifty eyes and a flabby lower lip.

"I want twenty dollars on the old man. Ken I have it?"

I rather expected that the bank would go into "action front," but the clerk said, "Certainly," and completed this rather odd financial transaction, whereat the bull-hunter stumbled out.

A CRACKER COWBOY

" Who is the old man in this case ?" I ventured.

" Oh, it's his boss, old Colonel Zuigg, of Crow City. I gave some money to some of his boys some weeks ago, and when the colonel was down here I asked him if he wanted the boys to draw against him in that way, and he said, ' Yes—for a small amount; they will steal a cow or two, and pay me that way.'"

Here was something tangible.

" What happens when a man steals another man's brand in this country ?"

" He mustn't get caught; that's all. They all do it, but they never bring their troubles into court. They just shoot it out there in the bresh. The last time old Colonel Zuigg brought Zorn Zuidden in here and had him indicted for stealing cattle, said Zorn: ' Now see here, old man Zuigg, what do you want for to go and git me arrested fer? I have stole thousands of cattle and put your mark and brand on 'em, and jes because I have stole a couple of hundred from you, you go and have me indicted. You jes better go and get that whole deal nol prossed;' and it was done."

The argument was perfect.

" From that I should imagine that the cow-people have no more idea of law than the ' gray apes,'" I commented.

" Yes, that's about it. Old Colonel Zuigg was a judge fer a spell, till some feller filled him with buckshot, and he had to resign ; and I remember he decided a case aginst me once. I was hot about it, and the old colonel he saw I was. Says he, ' Now yer mad, ain't you ?' And I allowed I was. ' Well,' says he, 'you hain't got no call to get mad. I have decided the last eight cases in yer favor, and you kain't have it go yer way all the time ; it wouldn't look right;' and I had to be satisfied."

The courts in that locality were but the faint and sickly flame of a taper offered at the shrine of a justice which was traditional only, it seemed. Moral forces having ceased to operate, the large owners began to brand everything in sight, never realizing that they were sowing the wind. This action naturally demoralized the cowboys, who shortly began to brand a little on their own account—and then the deluge. The rights of property having been destroyed, the large owners put strong outfits in the field, composed of desperate men armed to the teeth, and what happens in the lonely pine woods no one knows but the desperadoes themselves, albeit some of them never come back to the little fringe of settlements. The winter visitor from the North kicks up the jack-snipe along the beach or tarponizes in the estuaries of

FIGHTING OVER A STOLEN HERD

the Gulf, and when he comes to the hotel for dinner he eats Chicago dressed beef, but out in the
wilderness low-browed cow-folks shoot and stab
each other for the possession of scrawny creatures
not fit for a pointer-dog to mess on. One cannot
but feel the force of Buckle's law of " the physical
aspects of nature " in this sad country. Flat and
sandy, with miles on miles of straight pine timber,
each tree an exact duplicate of its neighbor tree,
and underneath the scrub palmettoes, the twisted
brakes and hammocks, and the gnarled water-oaks
festooned with the sad gray Spanish-moss—truly
not a country for a high-spirited race or moral
giants.

The land gives only a tough wiregrass, and the
poor little cattle, no bigger than a donkey, wander
half starved and horribly emaciated in search of
it. There used to be a trade with Cuba, but now
that has gone; and beyond the supplying of Key
West and the small fringe of settlements they
have no market. How well the cowboys serve
their masters I can only guess, since the big
owners do not dare go into the woods, or even to
their own doors at night, and they do not keep
a light burning in the houses. One, indeed, attempted to assert his rights, but some one pumped sixteen buckshot into him as he bent over a
spring to drink, and he left the country. They

do tell of a late encounter between two rival fore-
men, who rode on to each other in the woods, and
drawing, fired, and both were found stretched
dying under the palmettoes, one calling delirious-
ly the name of his boss. The unknown reaches
of the Everglades lie just below, and with a half-
hour's start a man who knew the country would
be safe from pursuit, even if it were attempted;
and, as one man cheerfully confided to me, "A
boat don't leave no trail, stranger."

That might makes right, and that they steal by
wholesale, any cattle-hunter will admit; and why
they brand at all I cannot see, since one boy tried
to make it plain to me, as he shifted his body in
drunken abandon and grabbed my pencil and a
sheet of wrapping paper: "See yer; ye see that?"
And he drew a circle **O**, and then another ring
around it, thus: **◎**. "That brand ain't no good.
Well, then—" And again his knotted and dirty
fingers essayed the brand **| O**. He laboriously
drew upon it and made **EΘ** which of course
destroyed the former brand.

"Then here," he continued, as he drew 13, "all
ye've got ter do is this—313." I gasped in amaze-
ment, not at his cleverness as a brand-destroyer,
but at his honest abandon. With a horrible op-

IN WAIT FOR AN ENEMY

eratic laugh, such as is painted in "The Cossack's Answer," he again laboriously drew ⊕ (the circle cross), and then added some marks which made it look like this : ⟨symbol⟩. And again breaking into his devil's "ha, ha!" said, "Make the damned thing whirl."

I did not protest. He would have shot me for that. But I did wish he was living in the northwest quarter of New Mexico, where Mr. Cooper and Dan could throw their eyes over the trail of his pony. Of course each man has adjusted himself to this lawless rustling, and only calculates that he can steal as much as his opponent. It is rarely that their affairs are brought to court, but when they are, the men come *en masse* to the room, armed with knives and rifles, so that any decision is bound to be a compromise, or it will bring on a general engagement.

There is also a noticeable absence of negroes among them, as they still retain some *ante bellum* theories, and it is only very lately that they have "reconstructed." Their general ignorance is "miraculous," and quite mystifying to an outside man. Some whom I met did not even know where the Texas was which furnishes them their ponies. The railroads of Florida have had their ups and downs with them in a petty way on account of the running over of their cattle by the trains; and then some long - haired old Cracker drops into the nearest station with his gun and pistol, and wants the telegraph operator to settle immediately on the basis of the Cracker's claim for damages, which is always absurdly high. At first the railroads demurred, but the cowboys lined up in the " bresh " on some dark night and pumped Winchesters into the train in a highly picturesque way. The trainmen at once recognized the force of the Cracker's views on cattle-killing, but it took some considerable " potting " at the more conservative superintendents before the latter could bestir themselves and invent a " cow-attorney," as the company adjuster is called, who now settles with the bushmen as best he can. Certainly no worse people ever lived since the big killing up Muscleshell way, and the romance is taken out of it by the cowardly assassination which is the practice. They are well paid for their desperate work, and always eat fresh beef or " razor-backs," and deer which they kill in the woods. The heat, the poor grass, their brutality, and the pest of the flies kill their ponies, and, as a rule, they lack dash and are indifferent riders, but they are picturesque in their unkempt, almost unearthly wildness. A strange effect is added by their use of large, fierce cur-dogs, one of which

A BIT OF COW COUNTRY

accompanies each cattle-hunter, and is taught to pursue cattle, and to even take them by the nose, which is another instance of their brutality. Still, as they only have a couple of horses apiece, it saves them much extra running. These men do not use the rope, unless to noose a pony in a corral, but work their cattle in strong log corrals, which are made at about a day's march apart all through the woods. Indeed, ropes are hardly necessary, since the cattle are so small and thin that two men can successfully "wrestle" a three-year-old. A man goes into the corral, grabs a cow by one horn, and throwing his other arm over her back, waits until some other man takes her hind leg, whereat ensues some very entertaining Græco-Roman style.

When the cow is successful, she finds her audience of Cracker cowboys sitting on the fence awaiting another opening, and gasping for breath. The best bull will not go over three hundred pounds, while I have seen a yearling at a hundred and fifty —if you, O knights of the riata, can imagine it! Still, it is desperate work. Some of the men are so reckless and active that they do not hesitate to encounter a wild bull in the open. The cattle are as wild as deer, they race off at scent; and when "rounded up" many will not drive, whereupon these are promptly shot. It frequently happens that when the herd is being driven quietly along a bull will turn on the drivers, charging at once. Then there is a scamper and great shooting. The bulls often become so maddened in these forays that they drop and die in their tracks, for which strange fact no one can account, but as a rule they are too scrawny and mean to make their handling difficult.

So this is the Cracker cowboy, whose chief interest would be found in the tales of some bush-whacking enterprise, which I very much fear would be a one-sided story, and not worth the telling. At best they must be revolting, having no note of the savage encounters which used to characterize the easy days in West Texas and New Mexico, when every man tossed his life away to the crackle of his own revolver. The moon shows pale through the leafy canopy on their evening fires, and the mists, the miasma, and the mosquitoes settle over their dreary camp talk. In place of the wild stampede, there is only the bellowing in the pens, and instead of the plains shaking under the dusty air as the bedizened vaqueros plough their fiery broncos through the milling herds, the cattle-hunter wends his lonely way through the ooze and rank grass, while the dreary pine trunks line up and shut the view.

COWBOYS WRESTLING A BULL

THE STRANGE DAYS THAT
CAME TO JIMMIE FRIDAY

———————

The " Abwee - chemun " * Club was organized
with six charter members at a heavy lunch in the
Savarin restaurant—one of those lunches which
make through connections to dinner without
change. One member basely deserted, while two
more lost all their enthusiasm on the following
morning, but three of us stuck. We vaguely knew
that somewhere north of the Canadian Pacific and
south of Hudson Bay were big lakes and rapid
rivers—lakes whose names we did not know; lakes
bigger than Champlain, with unnamed rivers between them. We did not propose to be boated
around in a big birch-bark by two voyagers among
blankets and crackers and ham, but each provided
himself a little thirteen-foot cedar canoe, twenty-
nine inches in the beam, and weighing less than

———————

* Algonquin for " paddle and canoe."

forty pounds. I cannot tell you precisely how our party was sorted, but one was a lawyer with eye-glasses and settled habits, loving nature, though detesting canoes; the other was nominally a merchant, but in reality an atavic Norseman of the wolf and raven kind; while I am not new. Together we started.

Presently the Abwees sat about the board of a lumbermen's hotel, filled with house-flies and slatternly waiter-girls, who talked familiarly while they served greasy food. The Abwees were yet sore in their minds at the thoughts of the smelly beds up-stairs, and discouragement sat deeply on their souls. But their time was not yet.

After breakfast they marched to the Hudson Bay Company's store, knowing as they did that in Canada there are only two places for a traveller to go who wants anything—the great company or the parish priest; and then, having explained to the factor their dream, they were told "that beyond, beyond some days' journey"—oh! that awful beyond, which for centuries has stood across the path of the pioneer, and in these latter days confronts the sportsman and wilderness-lover—"that beyond some days' journey to the north was a country such as they had dreamed—up Temiscamingue and beyond."

The subject of a guide was considered.

Jimmie Friday always brought a big toboggan-load of furs into Fort Tiemogamie every spring, and was accounted good in his business. He and his big brother trapped together, and in turn followed the ten days' swing through the snow-laden forest which they had covered with their dead-falls and steel-jawed traps; but when the ice went out in the rivers, and the great pines dripped with the melting snows, they had nothing more to do but cut a few cords of wood for their widowed mother's cabin near the post. Then the brother and he paddled down to Bais des Pierres, where the brother engaged as a deck hand on a steamboat, and Jimmie hired himself as a guide for some bush-rangers, as the men are called who explore for pine lands for the great lumber firms. Having worked all summer and got through with that business, Jimmie bethought him to dissipate for a few days in the bustling lumber town down on the Ottawa River. He had been there before to feel the exhilaration of civilization, but beyond that clearing he had never known anything more inspiring than a Hudson Bay post, which is generally a log store, a house where the agent lives, and a few tiny Indian cabins set higgledy-piggledy in a sunburnt gash of stumps and bowlders, lost in the middle of the solemn, unresponsive forest. On this morning in question he had stepped from his friend's cabin up in the Indian village, and after lighting a perfectly round and rather yellow cigar, he had instinctively wandered down to the Hudson Bay store, there to find himself amused by a strange sight.

The Abwees had hired two French-Indian voyagers of sinister mien, and a Scotch-Canadian boy bred to the bush. They were out on the grass, engaged in taking burlaps off three highly polished canoes, while the clerk from the store ran out and asked questions about " how much bacon," and, " will fifty pounds of pork be enough, sir?"

The round yellow cigar was getting stubby, while Jimmie's modest eyes sought out the points of interest in the new-comers, when he was suddenly and sharply addressed:

" Can you cook?"

Jimmie couldn't do anything in a hurry, except chop a log in two, paddle very fast, and shoot quickly, so he said, as was his wont:

" I think—I dun'no'—"

" Well, how much?" came the query.

" Two daul—ars—" said Jimmie.

The transaction was complete. The yellow butt went over the fence, and Jimmie shed his coat. He was directed to lend a hand by the bustling sportsmen, and requested to run and find things of which he had never before in his life heard the name.

"THE LAWYER HAD BECOME A VOYAGER"

After two days' travel the Abwees were put ashore — boxes, bags, rolls of blankets, canoes, Indians, and plunder of many sorts—on a pebbly beach, and the steamer backed off and steamed away. They had reached the "beyond" at last, and the odoriferous little bedrooms, the bustle of the preparation, the cares of their lives, were behind. Then there was a girding up of the loins, a getting out of tump-lines and canvas packs, and the long portage was begun.

The voyagers carried each two hundred pounds as they stalked away into the wilderness, while the attorney-at-law "hefted" his pack, wiped his eye-glasses with his pocket-handkerchief, and tried cheerfully to assume the responsibilities of "a dead game sport."

"I cannot lift the thing, and how I am going to carry it is more than I know; but I'm a dead game sport, and I am going to try. I do not want to be dead game, but it looks as though I couldn't help it. Will some gentleman help me to adjust this cargo?"

The night overtook the outfit in an old beaver meadow half-way through the trail. Like all first camps, it was tough. The lean-to tents went up awkwardly. No one could find anything. Late at night the Abwees lay on their backs under the blankets, while the fog settled over the meadow and blotted out the stars.

On the following day the stuff was all gotten through, and by this time the lawyer had become a voyager, willing to carry anything he could stagger under. It is strange how one can accustom himself to "pack." He may never use the tump-line, since it goes across the head, and will unseat his intellect if he does, but with shoulder-straps and a tump-line a man who thinks he is not strong will simply amaze himself inside of a week by what he can do. As for our little canoes, we could trot with them. Each Abwee carried his own belongings and his boat, which entitled him to the distinction of "a dead game sport," whatever that may mean, while the Indians portaged their larger canoes and our mass of supplies, making many trips backward and forward in the process.

At the river everything was parcelled out and arranged. The birch-barks were repitched, and every man found out what he was expected to portage and do about camp. After breaking and making camp three times, the outfit could pack up, load the canoes, and move inside of fifteen minutes. At the first camp the lawyer essayed his canoe, and was cautioned that the delicate thing might flirt with him. He stepped in and sat gracefully down in about two feet of water, while the "delicate thing" shook herself saucily at his side. After he had crawled dripping ashore and wiped his eye-

"IT IS STRANGE HOW ONE CAN ACCUSTOM
HIMSELF TO 'PACK'"

glasses, he engaged to sell the "delicate thing" to an Indian for one dollar and a half on a promissory note. The trade was suppressed, and he was urged to try again. A man who has held down a cane-bottom chair conscientiously for fifteen years looks askance at so fickle a thing as a canoe twenty-nine inches in the beam. They are nearly as hard to sit on in the water as a cork; but once one is in the bottom they are stable enough, though they do not submit to liberties or palsied movements. The staid lawyer was filled with horror at the prospect of another go at his polished beauty; but remembering his resolve to be dead game, he abandoned his life to the chances, and got in this time safely.

So the Abwees went down the river on a golden morning, their double-blade paddles flashing the sun and sending the drip in a shower on the glassy water. The smoke from the lawyer's pipe hung behind him in the quiet air, while the note of the reveille clangored from the little buglette of the Norseman. Jimmie and the big Scotch backwoodsman swayed their bodies in one boat, while the two sinister voyagers dipped their paddles in the big canoe.

The Norseman's gorge came up, and he yelled back: "Say! this suits me. I am never going back to New York."

Jimmie grinned at the noise; it made him happy. Such a morning, such a water, such a lack of anything to disturb one's peace! Let man's better nature revel in the beauties of existence; they inflate his soul. The colors play upon the senses—the reddish-yellow of the birch-barks, the blue of the water, and the silver sheen as it parts at the bows of the canoes; the dark evergreens, the steely rocks with their lichens, the white trunks of the birches, their fluffy tops so greeny green, and over all the gold of a sunny day. It is my religion, this thing, and I do not know how to tell all I feel concerning it.

The rods were taken out, a gang of flies put on and trolled behind—but we have all seen a man fight a five-pound bass for twenty minutes. The waters fairly swarmed with them, and we could always get enough for the "pot" in a half-hour's fishing at any time during the trip. The Abwees were canoeing, not hunting or fishing; though, in truth, they did not need to hunt spruce-partridge or fish for bass in any sporting sense; they simply went out after them, and never stayed over half an hour. On a point we stopped for lunch: the Scotchman always struck the beach a-cooking. He had a "kit," which was a big camp-pail, and inside of it were more dishes than are to be found in some hotels. He broiled the bacon, instead of

"DOWN THE RIVER ON A GOLDEN MORNING"

frying it, and thus we were saved the terrors of indigestion. He had many luxuries in his commissary, among them dried apples, with which he filled a camp-pail one day and put them on to boil. They subsequently got to be about a foot deep all over the camp, while Furguson stood around and regarded the black-magic of the thing with overpowering emotions and Homeric tongue. Furguson was a good genius, big and gentle, and a woodsman root and branch. The Abwees had intended their days in the wilderness to be happy singing flights of time, but with grease and paste in one's stomach what may not befall the mind when it is bent on nature's doings?

And thus it was that the gloomy Indian Jimmie Friday, despite his tuberculosis begotten of insufficient nourishment, was happy in these strange days—even to the extent of looking with wondrous eyes on the nooks which we loved—nooks which previously for him had only sheltered possible "dead-falls" or not, as the discerning eye of the trapper decided the prospects for pelf.

Going ashore on a sandy beach, Jimmie wandered down its length, his hunter mind seeking out the footprints of his prey. He stooped down, and then beckoned me to come, which I did.

Pointing at the sand, he said, "You know him?"

"Wolves," I answered.

"Yes—first time I see 'em up here—they be follerin' the deers—bad—bad. No can trap 'em— verrie smart."

A half-dozen wolves had chased a deer into the water; but wolves do not take to the water, so they had stopped and drank, and then gone rollicking together up the beach. There were cubs, and one great track as big as a mastiff might make.

"See that—moose track—he go by yesterday;" and Jimmie pointed to enormous footprints in the muck of a marshy place. "Verrie big moose—we make call at next camp—think it is early for call."

At the next camp Jimmie made the usual birch-bark moose-call, and at evening blew it, as he also did on the following morning. This camp was a divine spot on a rise back of a long sandy beach, and we concluded to stop for a day. The Norseman and I each took a man in our canoes and started out to explore. I wanted to observe some musk-rat hotels down in a big marsh, and the Norseman was fishing. The attorney was content to sit on a log by the shores of the lake, smoke lazily, and watch the sun shimmer through the lifting fog. He saw a canoe approaching from across the lake. He gazed vacantly at it, when it grew strange and more unlike a canoe. The paddles did not move, but the phantom craft drew quickly on.

A REAL CAMP

"Say, Furguson — come here — look at that canoe."

The Scotchman came down, with a pail in one hand, and looked. "Canoe—hell—it's a moose— and there ain't a pocket-pistol in this camp," and he fairly jumped up and down.

"You don't say—you really don't say!" gasped the lawyer, who now began to exhibit signs of insanity.

"Yes—he's going to be d——d sociable with us —he's coming right bang into this camp."

The Indian too came down, but he was long past talking English, and the gutturals came up in lumps, as though he was trying to keep them down.

The moose finally struck a long point of sand and rushes about two hundred yards away, and drew majestically out of the water, his hide dripping, and the sun glistening on his antlers and back.

The three men gazed in spellbound admiration at the picture until the moose was gone. When they had recovered their senses they slowly went up to the camp on the ridge—disgusted and dumfounded.

"I could almost put a cartridge in that old guncase and kill him," sighed the backwoodsman.

"I have never hunted in my life," mused the

attorney, "but few men have seen such a sight," and he filled his pipe.

"Hark — listen!" said the Indian. There was a faint cracking, which presently became louder. "He's coming into camp;" and the Indian nearly died from excitement as he grabbed a hatchet. The three unfortunate men stepped to the back of the tents, and as big a bull moose as walks the lonely woods came up to within one hundred and fifty feet of the camp, and stopped, returning their gaze.

Thus they stood for what they say was a minute, but which seemed like hours. The attorney composedly admired the unusual sight. The Indian and Furguson swore softly but most viciously until the moose moved away. The Indian hurled the hatchet at the retreating figure, with a final curse, and the thing was over.

"Those fellows who are out in their canoes will be sick abed when we tell them what's been going on in the camp this morning," sighed Mr. Furguson, as he scoured a cooking-pot.

I fear we would have had that moose on our consciences if we had been there: the game law was not up at the time, but I should have asked for strength from a higher source than my respect for law.

The golden days passed and the lake grew great.

ROUGH WATER

The wind blew at our backs. The waves rolled in restless surges, piling the little canoes on their crests and swallowing them in the troughs. The canoes thrashed the water as they flew along, half in, half out, but they rode like ducks. The Abwees took off their hats, gripped their double blades, made the water swirl behind them, howled in glee to each other through the rushing storm. To be five miles from shore in a seaway in kayaks like ours was a sensation. We found they stood it well, and grew contented. It was the complement to the golden lazy days when the water was glass, and the canoes rode upsidedown over its mirror surface. The Norseman grinned and shook his head in token of his pleasure, much as an epicure might after a sip of superior Burgundy.

" How do you fancy this?" we asked the attorney-at-law.

" I am not going to deliver an opinion until I get ashore. I would never have believed that I would be here at my time of life, but one never knows what a —— fool one can make of one's self. My glasses are covered with water, and I can hardly see, but I can't let go of this paddle to wipe them," shrieked the man of the office chair, in the howl of the weather.

But we made a long journey by the aid of the wind, and grew a contempt for it. How could one imagine the stability of those little boats until one had tried it?

That night we put into a natural harbor and camped on a gravel beach. The tents were up and the supper cooking, when the wind hauled and blew furiously into our haven. The fires were scattered and the rain came in blinding sheets. The tent-pegs pulled from the sand. We sprang to our feet and held on to the poles, wet to the skin. It was useless; the rain blew right under the canvas. We laid the tents on the "grub" and stepped out into the dark. We could not be any wetter, and we did not care. To stand in the dark in the wilderness, with nothing to eat, and a fire-engine playing a hose on you for a couple of hours —if you have imagination enough, you can fill in the situation. But the gods were propitious. The wind died down. The stars came out by myriads. The fires were relighted, and the ordinary life begun. It was late in the night before our clothes, blankets, and tents were dry, but, like boys, we forgot it all.

Then came a river—blue and flat like the sky above—running through rushy banks, backed by the masses of the forest; anon the waters rushed upon us over the rocks, and we fought, plunk-plunk-plunk, with the paddles, until our strength gave out. We stepped out into the water, and

"THE INDIANS USED 'SETTING-POLES'"

getting our lines, and using our long double blades as fenders, "tracked" the canoes up through the boil. The Indians in their heavier boats used "setting-poles" with marvellous dexterity, and by furious exertion were able to draw steadily up the grade—though at times they too "tracked," and even portaged. Our largest canoe weighed two hundred pounds, but a little voyager managed to lug it, though how I couldn't comprehend, since his pipe-stem legs fairly bent and wobbled under the enormous ark. None of us by this time were able to lift the loads which we carried, but, like a Western pack-mule, we stood about and had things piled on to us, until nothing more would stick. Some of the backwoodsmen carry incredible masses of stuff, and their lore is full of tales which no one could be expected to believe. Our men did not hesitate to take two hundred and fifty pounds over short portages, which were very rough and stony, though they all said if they slipped they expected to break a leg. This is largely due to the tump-line, which is laid over the head, while persons unused to it must have shoulder-straps in addition, which are not as good, because the "breastbone," so called, is not strong enough.

We were getting day by day farther into "the beyond." There were no traces here of the hand of man. Only Jimmie knew the way—it was his trapping - ground. Only once did we encounter people. We were blown into a little board dock, on a gray day, with the waves piling up behind us, and made a difficult landing. Here were a few tiny log houses—an outpost of the Hudson Bay Company. We renewed our stock of provisions, after laborious trading with the stagnated people who live in the lonely place. There was nothing to sell us but a few of the most common necessities; however, we needed only potatoes and sugar. This was Jimmie's home. Here we saw his poor old mother, who was being tossed about in the smallest of canoes as she drew her nets. Jimmie's father had gone on a hunting expedition and had never come back. Some day Jimmie's old mother will go out on the wild lake to tend her nets, and she will not come back. Some time Jimmie too will not return—for this Indian struggle with nature is appalling in its fierceness.

There was a dance at the post, which the boys attended, going by canoe at night, and they came back early in the morning, with much giggling at their gallantries.

The loneliness of this forest life is positively discouraging to think about. What the long winters must be in the little cabins I cannot imagine, and I fear the traders must be all avarice, or have none at all; for there can certainly be

TRYING MOMENTS

absolutely no intellectual life. There is undoubtedly work, but not one single problem concerning
it. The Indian hunters do fairly well in a financial
way, though their lives are beset with weakening
hardships and constant danger. Their meagre
diet wears out their constitutions, and they are
subject to disease. The simplicity of their minds
makes it very difficult to see into their life as they
try to narrate it to one who may be interested.

From here on was through beautiful little lakes,
and the voyagers rigged blanket sails on the big
canoes, while we towed behind. Then came the
river and the rapids, which we ran, darting between
rocks, bumping on sunken stones—shooting fairly
out into the air, all but turning over hundreds of
times. One day the Abwees glided out in the big
lake Tesmiaquemang, and saw the steamer going
to Bais des Pierres. We hailed her, and she
stopped, while the little canoes danced about in
the swell as we were loaded one by one. On the
deck above us the passengers admired a kind of
boat the like of which had not before appeared in
these parts.

At Bais des Pierres we handed over the residue
of the commissaries of the Abwee-Chemun to
Jimmie Friday, including personally many pairs of
well-worn golf-breeches, sweaters, rubber coats,
knives which would be proscribed by law in New

York. If Jimmie ever parades his solemn wilderness in these garbs, the owls will laugh from the trees. Our simple forest friend laid in his winter stock—traps, flour, salt, tobacco, and pork, a new axe—and accompanied us back down the lake again on the steamer. She stopped in mid-stream, while Jimmie got his bundles into his "bark" and shoved off, amid a hail of "good-byes."

The engine palpitated, the big wheel churned the water astern, and we drew away. Jimmie bent on his paddle with the quick body-swing habitual to the Indian, and after a time grew a speck on the reflection of the red sunset in Temiscamingue.

The Abwees sat sadly leaning on the after-rail, and agreed that Jimmie was "a lovely Injun." Jimmie had gone into the shade of the overhang of the cliffs, when the Norseman started violently up, put his hands in his pockets, stamped his foot, said, " By George, fellows, any D. F. would call this a sporting trip !"

THE SOLEDAD GIRLS

"To-night I am going down to my ranch—
the Soledad—in my private car," said the manager of the Mexican International Railroad, "and
I would like the Captain and you to accompany
me."

The Captain and I were only too glad; so in
process of time we awoke to find our car side-
tracked on the Soledad, which is in the state of
Coahuila, Mexico. The chaparral spread around,
rising and falling in the swell of the land, until it
beat against the blue ridge of the Sierra Santa
Rosa, miles to the north. Here and there the
bright sun spotted on a cow as she threaded the
gray stretches; a little coyote-wolf sat on his
haunches on a near-by hill-side, and howled pro-
tests at his new-found companions; while dimly
through the gray meshes of the leaf-denuded
chaparral we could see the main ranch-house of
the Soledad. We were informed at breakfast by
the railroad manager that there was to be that day

a " round-up," which is to say, a regular Buffalo
Bill Show, with real cowboys, ponies, and cattle,
all three of them wild, full of thorns, and just out
of the brush.

The negro porters got out the saddles of the
young women, thus disclosing their intention to
ride ponies instead of in traps. We already knew
that they were fearless horseback-riders, but when
the string of ponies which were to be our mounts
was led up by a few Mexicans, the Captain and I
had our well-concealed doubts about their being
proper sort of ponies for young girls to ride. We
confided in an imperturbable cowboy — one of
those dry Texans. He said : " Them are what we
would call broke ponies, and you fellers needn't
get to worryin' 'bout them little girls—you're jest
a-foolin' away good time." Nevertheless, the
broncos had the lurking devil in the tails of their
eyes as they stood there tied to the wire fencing ;
they were humble and dejected as only a bronco
or a mule can simulate. When that ilk look most
cast down, be not deceived, gay brother ; they are
not like this. Their humility is only humorous,
and intended to lure you on to their backs, where,
unless you have a perfect understanding of the
game, the joke will be on you. Instantly one is
mounted, the humility departs ; he plunges and
starts about, or sets off like the wind, regardless

of thorny bushes, tricky ground underfoot, or the seat of the rider.

The manager's wife came out of the car with her little brood of three, and then two visiting friends. These Soledad girls, as I call them, each had a sunburst of yellow hair, were well bronzed by the Mexican sun, and were sturdy little bodies. They were dressed in short skirts, with leggings, topped with Tam o' Shanters, while about their waists were cartridge-belts, with delicate knives and revolvers attached, and with spurs and *quirts* as accessories. They took up their men's saddles, for they rode astride, except the two visitors, who were older and more lately from Chicago. They swung their saddles on to the ponies, showing familiarity with the *ladigo* straps of the Texas saddles, and proudly escaping the humiliation which alights on the head of one who in the cow-camps cannot saddle his own "bronc." Being ready, we mounted, and followed a cowboy off down the road to the *rodeo*-ground. The manager and Madam Mamma rode in a buckboard, proudly following with their gaze the galloping ponies which bore their jewels. I thought they should be fearful for their safety, but after more intimate inspection, I could see how groundless was such solicitude.

I must have it understood that these little

vaquero girls were not the ordinary Texas product, fed on corn-meal and bred in the chaparral,
but the much looked after darlings of a fond
mother. They are taken South every winter, that
their bodies may be made lithe and healthy, but
at the same time two or more governesses crowd
their minds with French, German, and other
things with which proper young girls should be
acquainted. But their infant minds did not carry
back to the days when they had not felt a horse
under them. To be sure, in the beginning it was
only a humble donkey, but even before they knew
they had graduated to ponies, and while yet ten
years old, it was only by a constant watch that
they were kept off unbroken broncos—horses that
made the toughest vaqueros throw down their hats,
tighten their belts, and grin with fear.

From over the hills came the half-wild cattle,
stringing along at a trot, all bearing for the open
space in the waste of the chaparral where the *rodeo*
occurred, while behind them followed the cowboys
—gay desert figures with brown, pinched faces,
long hair, and shouting wild cries. The exhilaration of the fine morning, the tramp of the thousands,
got into the curls of the three little Misses Golden-
hairs, and they scurried away, while I followed to
feast on this fresh vision, where absolutely ideal
little maids shouted Spanish at murderous-looking

"THE HALF-WILD CATTLE CAME DOWN FROM THE HILLS"

Mexican cow-punchers done up in bright serapes and costumed out of all reason. As the vaqueros dashed about hither and thither to keep their herds moving in the appointed direction, the infants screamed in their childish treble and spurred madly too. A bull stands at bay, but a child dashes at him, while he turns and flees. It is not their first *rodeo*, one can see, but I should wish they were with mamma and the buckboard, instead of out here in the brush, charging wild bulls, though in truth this never were written. These bulls frequently charge men, and a cow-pony turns like a ball off a bat, and a slippery seat in the saddle may put you under the feet of the outraged monarch of the range.

Driving down to the *rodeo*-ground, we all stood about on our ponies and held the herd, as it is called, the young girls doing vaquero duty, as imperturbable of mien as Mr. Flannagan, the foreman. So many women in the world are afraid of a dairy cow, even gathering up their skirts and preparing to shriek at the sight of one eating daisies. But these young women will grow up and they will be afraid of no cow. So much for a Soledad education.

The top-ropers rode slowly into the dust of the milling herd, scampered madly, cast their ropes, and came jumping to us with a blatting calf trailing at their ropes' end. Two men seized the little victim, threw him on his back, cut a piece out of his ear with a knife, and still held him in relentless grip while another pressed a red-hot branding-iron on his side, which sizzled and sent up blue smoke, together with an odor of burned flesh. The calves bawled piteously. There was no more emotion on the faces of the Soledad girls than was shown by the brown cowboys. They had often, very often, seen this before, and their nerves were strong. Some day I can picture in my mind's eye these young girl vaqueros grown to womanhood, and being such good-looking creatures, very naturally some young man will want very badly to marry one of them—for it cannot be otherwise. I only hope he will not be a thin-chested, cigarette-smoking dude, because it will be a sacrilege of nature. He must undoubtedly have played forward at Princeton or Yale, or be unworthy.

As we stood, a massive bull emerged from the body of the herd, his head thrown high, tail stiff with anger, eye rolling, and breath coming quick. He trotted quickly forward, and, lowering his head, charged through the "punchers." Instantly a small Soledad girl was after him, the vaqueros reining back to enjoy the strange ride with their eyes. Her hat flew off, and the long curls flapped in the rushing air as her pony fairly sailed over the difficult ground. The bull tore furiously, but behind him swept the pony and the child. As we watched, the chase had gone a mile away, but little Miss Yellowcurls drew gradually to the far side of the bull, quartering him on the far side, and whirling on, headed her quarry back to her audience and the herd. The rough-and-ready American range boss sat sidewise in his saddle and thought —for he never talked unnecessarily, though appreciation was chalked all over his pose. The manager and madam felt as though they were responsible for this wonderful thing. The Mexican cowboys snapped their fingers and eyes at one another, shouting quick Spanish, while the American part of the beholders agreed that it was the "limit'; "that as a picture," etc.; "that the American girl, properly environed"; "that this girl in particular," etc., was a dream. Then the bull and the girl came home; the bull to his fellows, and the girl to us. But she didn't have an idea of our admiration, because we didn't tell her; that would have been wrong, as you can imagine. Ten years will complicate little Miss Yellowcurls. Then she could be vain about such a thing; but, alas! she will not be—she will have forgotten.

THE END